The Pied Wizard of Regis Towne

by

Laura Strickland

Fairy Tales Retold

The Pied Wizard of Regis Towne

Cover Art by *Diana Carlile*

The Wild Rose Press, Inc.
PO Box 708
Adams Basin, NY 14410-0708
Visit us at www.thewildrosepress.com

Publishing History
First Edition, 2022
Trade Paperback ISBN 978-1-5092-4245-0
Digital ISBN 978-1-5092-4246-7

Fairy Tales Retold
Published in the United States of America

Dedication

For all those who refuse to tolerate injustice

Chapter One

Allow me to confide a small secret. Once upon a time, I was a Rat.

This was in the days when magic was alive in the world, an accepted part of life. In the Kingdom of Regis where I dwelt—as a Rat—there were high sorcerers who lived like kings and sacred mages who held more power than the priests. There were also hedge witches and lowly conjurers who traveled the land with their spells bundled onto their backs. And there were men like Timor Springerle, who sold their God-given powers for a profit along the way.

What has all that to do with me being once a Rat? For I am a Man now, as you can clearly see. Listen, and I will tell you the tale.

There was a plague in the land of Regis, in the spring of that year. Folk always fell sick in the winter with minor ailments like ague and dysentery. They took their tonics in the spring and grew stronger. But this particular spring the illness refused to clear.

Initially it struck the young, the children of the households. I lived then with my Mother and many brothers and sisters beneath the floorboards of one Christian Dobbs, a weaver. We could hear most of what went on through the boards above our heads, and aye, the children of that house did fall ill with a terrible fever and spots on their skin. Physicians came to poke

1

and prod at them. They said the fever spread throughout the town and was caused by us—Rats.

That is a bald-faced lie, as I will attest. It is true we did venture up into the house at night and sometimes during the day also if we were very hungry, in order to steal food. They did not have much. The pickings were slim in Regis among the poor.

But we did not carry the plague—the fleas that beset us did. A Rat cannot help having fleas, can he? No more than he can keep those fleas from biting men.

Once word spread, however, as you can imagine, we were persecuted. Men came with terriers and ferrets, but many of us had strong hiding places beneath the town, and those pests could not reach us. Many of my kind died, but the Men could not find us all.

Children continued to suffer and perish.

Mother squeaked to us fiercely about keeping our noses down and staying out of sight. We near-starved for a while. The town, though, was full of Rats, and as I heard it explained later, the lord mayor and the town council were pressed to do something about it.

Enter Timor Springerle.

Timor, as I later came to call him, was what was known as a chancer. Of perhaps thirty human years, he'd traveled extensively and garnered for himself a reputation. He was said to be the Man who could solve the town of Regis' Rat problem.

I learned some of what transpired by listening to the family whose house we occupied, through those floorboards. And some from the Man himself after what transpired—well, did transpire.

He did have magic, did Timor Springerle. Let that be admitted. But even though he called himself a wizard, it was an underhanded kind of magic, founded in the gutter, so to speak. He knew some spells, but as will be seen, he did not do a good job of using them. He was a messy magician, and a careless wizard. He squandered much in the casting.

The first warning we had of disaster brewing came when old Grandfather Beak called us all together for a meet-and-squeak. An ancient Rat was Beak, a true survivor, and actually my many-times grandsire. Rats are not particularly sophisticated creatures, though we're canny when it comes to survival and will do most anything we must to stay alive.

I was at this time a fully grown male Rat with many younger siblings. I would have left the nest had there been anywhere to go, and had ventured out into the city upon occasion. Other Rats held the territory around us, many other Rats. After getting into squabbles and bite-fights a few times, I always returned home.

I was well past what you might call the age of obedience, and when old Beak summoned us I went more out of curiosity than anything else.

The space beneath the floorboards of the house had become a warren. Spaces between the joists had been chewed and altered by generations of Rats and made into larger chambers. We congregated beneath what would be the kitchen, upstairs.

"Listen to me, all of you," Grandfather Beak commanded. "Quieten down, now."

The youngsters, nipped by their Mothers, quieted.

"The Men want rid of us. Well, they've always wanted rid of us, haven't they?"

Every young Rat was brought up knowing this.

Men would do whatever they could to eradicate our kind. To survive, we must keep clear of their traps, their poisons, and their great feet.

"They're blaming us for this plague that besets them, even though it's all down to those fleas." Grandfather nipped irritably at his flank. "Can we help it if they like to bite Men as well as us?"

Rats rarely bit Men. Dogs did, far more often, and even cats, though humans tolerated the presence of both in their lives. A Rat might bite a Man if cornered and desperate to escape. An act of fear it was. I'd been told Men tasted bad, indeed.

"Word has come down," Grandfather Beak said. "A Man has been hired by the town to eradicate us."

Eradicate. A terrible word. It brought to mind all the dreadful things Men had done to us in the past in comparison with which, quite honestly, an occasional nip scarcely seemed equal.

"This Man will employ magic against us."

Everyone listening murmured. Rats believed in magic—well, back then, as I say, most the world did. I could not remember whether I'd ever before heard of magic being employed against Rats. Nearly every other method of destruction had.

"What kind of magic?" asked one of the many Mother Rats.

"Rat magic, I suppose," Beak murmured. "Lure magic. Some sort of spell he will cast. I am not certain. So you must be on guard and strive to resist it when it comes."

Resist magic? Could it be done? I was a brave enough Rat. I feared little, but a shiver passed through me now and set all my hair aquiver.

Danger.

"How do we resist?" another Mother squeaked in distress.

"I am not sure, for I know not what form the magic will take. The Council of Grandfathers merely says we should make sure all our underlings are prepared."

The Council of Grandfathers, made up of the most ancient surviving Rats of Regis, rarely set down such edicts, being only loosely united.

"Oh dear, oh dear," the same Mother squeaked. "I have a score of children to care for. Will we all die?"

"Daughter, I cannot say. I can advise you only that, when you feel the magic, you must fight against it."

"Why will the Men do this terrible thing to us?" cried another Rat, one of my cousins.

"Fear," said Grandfather Beak. "Fear creates hatred, which is the true enemy."

I disagreed with him. Hatred made you strong. Already I hated all Men and none so much as the wizard who threatened us.

****

We did not know when the blow would fall, which made the following days difficult. Uncertainty is a cruel master and an anathema to a peaceful existence.

In the days that followed, some Rats did foolish things like abandoning the house for the outer world. They must have thought they would be safer, though we'd all been taught from squeaklings that hunkering down in the dark kept us most secure.

Anyway, all of Regis would be subject to this spell, as I understood it. A Rat would have to run far in order to escape.

As I say, we mostly lay low and waited for the

blow to fall. Much more activity ensued upstairs. Physicians came in and out. They burned strange potions that made the air stink. Bodies were carried out. Prodigious weeping could be heard.

Rats do not weep. We chitter in distress sometimes, and when greatly grieved, we keen. The Men upstairs carried on in a most shocking fashion.

Times for us were lean. The Men had taken to putting their food away quite carefully. The master of the house shut his cheese away in a stone larder and hung his bread from the rafters in a net bag. Not even the most determined Rat could reach it.

I suppose we might all have starved if the Terrible Spell hadn't been cast. But happen it did, on a sunny Sunday afternoon.

Chapter Two

I could tell it was Sunday because the church bells rang out. I'd learned about church bells from Mother when, as a little squeaker, I inquired about sounds we could hear on only certain days.

"Why do you ask so many questions?" she complained. "Never has there been such a Rat for questions."

"I want to know."

"Certain Men's homes have big, clattering bells up top. They use them to summon others, the way the Grandfathers sometimes summon us."

"Why do they not just squeak?"

"Foolish Rat, Men do not squeak."

"Are the Men in danger?"

"No. On Sundays they come together to pray."

Rats did pray, in a fashion. We certainly didn't congregate to do it. But when the sole of a large boot descended upon a hapless Rat or he was cast into a flaming barrel, he did pray. Rats feel pain like anyone else. Never let that be doubted.

On this particular Sunday, the Men went to church and prayed for our deaths before setting Timor Springerle on us. In fact, they had their Sunday dinners first—those who could afford it—before coming outside to watch.

I felt the first threads of the magic early that

afternoon. Magic does indeed have threads. Spells are woven from intentions drawn out into tendrils some can see and most can feel. Deep beneath the floor of our Man's house, I could feel them.

It felt like an invisible hand reached up, not seeking to capture so much as entice me. Like a finger crooked in invitation, it drew upon my spirit, calling, calling me to follow it. Even though we'd been warned by the Grandfathers and by our Mothers, many of us went. The desire to do so compelled us. Claws scrabbled all around me as Rats climbed from their deep hiding places. They queued up to push through the openings that had been gnawed in discreet places, in the floor and walls, desperate to be up and out. Some of the Mothers squeaked to them, calling them back. Most gave in and went along. Did I go along? Let it be remembered I was a strong-minded Rat—as shall be later proven—a Rat in a thousand, so to speak. But the Rat magic proved stronger.

Magic would not be magic were it not compelling. That is the very definition of it—a compelling use of will. And Timor Springerle *could* cast a spell, however sloppy he might be about it.

The street flooded with Rats. All sizes, ages, and colors, they indeed flowed like water, headed each and every one in the same direction as the Rat magic bade them.

From the narrow street where stood the house I'd occupied all my life, we emptied into another larger street, one of the town's main thoroughfares. Here was what I can only call a river of Rats. I with my family members and neighbors pushed our way into it.

Driven, I could feel the need inside me to obey that

magic urge and could feel the corresponding compulsion in the Rats all around me. It felt like a terrible hunger with a promise behind it, a promise that the hunger would be assuaged if only we obeyed the call.

You can perhaps imagine what this was like. Furry bodies jostling all around me amid the heat of it, crowded so closely together. My companions chittered. They squeaked questions at one another…questions that went unanswered, for no one understood what drove them.

From where I was, I could not see the head of the line—could not tell if anyone led us. But I began to wonder if someone did not drive us from behind, and I wanted to know.

Slowly, bit by bit, I fell back. It was difficult to do, both because the compulsion bade me always forward, and because with the press of so many behind me, momentum held me in its grasp. I would like to think that, strong as the urge was, my will remained stronger.

I hung back. I wriggled, and the others went around me. In this way I let most of them pass and eventually found myself at the rear of the flood. This may well have saved my life.

I found no one back there save other stragglers, those with limps, the aged and the infirm. They lunged or hopped along, but no one drove them. I discovered no Rat shepherds, so to speak.

Many Men, though, stood out along our route staring. Householders stuck their heads through their doorways and gaped at the river of Rats.

I should have peeled off then, run back to our burrow beneath the house, which would be empty now, and silent. To tell the truth, I tried. But the Rat magic remained too strong.

I wondered where we were going. For we soon left the town proper and headed down toward the sea. Have I mentioned that Regis is a seaside town? A port on the broad Forth.

In fact, many of our ancestors had arrived here on ships long ago. Not that Rats like water. We can swim if we have to, but not well or for long. And we avoid the sea when we can.

Until now. The river of Rats veered sharply and like most rivers appeared ready to empty into the sea.

I protested the thought. So did many others of my company, and a great distressed cry arose from a multitude of Rat throats. That did not in any way impede the magic that continued to impel us forward.

To an aged, three-legged Rat beside me, who brought up of the tail of the horde, I said, "What is happening, Grandfather?"

He turned milky eyes on me. "It is a spell cast by a wizard. He will run us into the sea."

Sure enough, a line of docks fronted the harbor. Even as we ran forward, the first of us, spreading out, reached these and without pause or hesitation leaped off, as from a cliff.

"Resist, my son!" the ancient Rat called to me. "Resist!"

I wanted to. I could not. It was as if my paws had minds of their own, ones that had been enchanted. They scrabbled onward even though I ordered them to halt. Even though I knew what was happening up ahead. I could hear the squeaks and terrified cries of those who jumped from the stone docks, full of horror and distress. But they leaped anyway, just as I ran on.

The flood of Rats continued to move up steadily to the wide harbor front. The drag of my determined resistance made me one of the last.

I saw him then. standing to the left of us, Rats tumbling over his feet to get to the sea. A single Man standing tall and with a staff in his hand. Making no secret of what he was.

A wizard. Dressed in brightly colored clothing, he wore what I could only call a wizard's hat, tall and conical. He held his staff high up in the air, and the magic poured from it in a nearly visible current. Sending us to our deaths.

That wasn't all 1 could see. As we continued toward the harbor, I beheld the Rats ahead of us plunging into the sea, where they commenced to swim straight outward into the open water.

Rats can swim but not for long. These hundreds would soon tire. They would go under the oily green waves.

Some Rats balked when they saw those ahead of them swimming toward their deaths. They tried to hold back from the plunge, to turn the tide. The instinct to preserve one's life is very strong.

The Rat magic proved stronger. Seeing the Rats balk, the wizard raised his staff still higher and muttered some words. The compulsion increased. The Rats along the edge of the docks immediately ceased to resist and plunged over the side.

Grandfather Rat and I, the last of the group and hanging back, somehow missed being netted by that spell. Perhaps we escaped the wizard's eye, which he cast only so far. I know I trembled as I watched the river of Rats open up ahead of me, bodies gray, brown, and every shade of Rat going over the side.

"Resist," Grandfather Rat squeaked at me again.

I clung to him and he to me as if we believed combining our wills could be enough to save us. Still the magic edged us toward the dock, where I saw a terrible sight.

A furry current of Rats flowed out to sea. It looked just like a river might, emptying into the greater water. I could hear them, the splashing of their feet, their squeaks as they realized what occurred. Once they were in the water, the spell lifted from them. Those in the rear scrabbled against the stone wharves, but they could not climb back up. They might have climbed aboard any moored ships there in the harbor, but this betrayal had been well-planned. The harbor stood empty of vessels.

Those Rats out in front began losing their battle with exhaustion, and floundered. Their companions behind quickly followed.

And the wizard—he who stood above the harbor watching it all? He smiled.

All my family gone. Everyone I'd ever known dead. And this evil mage smiled.

A sob wracked the body of Grandfather Rat, whom I still clutched. For we were the only two—the only two left alive.

An even more terrible thing happened then. The wizard turned and saw us, two Rats alone, cowering against the stones of the pier. We must have looked very small to him. Insignificant. Yet his smile faded and a look of anger filled his eyes.

I'd seen anger in Men's faces before. Men did

horrid things to Rats when angered—stomped on them, clubbed them, or set them afire. I expected no mercy now, and indeed we received none.

Our resistance had taken us to the verge of the drop. Rats still swam and writhed below us in the water and died by their thousands. The wizard, not satisfied with this wholesale carnage, swore and swung at us with the butt of his staff, seeking to knock us into the water.

"I said all!"

Magic accompanied his words and lent his blows purpose. One swipe nearly had me—I scrabbled aside barely in time. The next almost took Grandfather.

The wizard exclaimed and swung his staff again. Thinking it must strike me and knock me over the side, I seized hold of it at the end, using both teeth and claws to hold on.

I felt a bright tingle of magic. It spread from my mouth, which gripped the staff, and to a lesser degree from my paws, and arced through me like pain. The shock of it almost made me let go, but the wizard swung the staff out over the water and tried to shake me off.

Grandfather Rat squeaked frantically. The wizard grunted and drew me in onto the stone. He shot a look back toward the town. The Men were coming. They approached at a hurried rate, Men in frock coats and hats—the officials of the town—and Men in workers' garb. This did not seem to please the wizard.

"I promised all!" he exclaimed more loudly and succeeded in shaking me from the staff. I landed beside Grandfather, and the Wizard glared at us.

"No rats," he said. He squinted his eyes, and I saw

they were pied—one green and one brown. The sight terrified me. For of all the awful stares I'd received from Men, this was the worst.

He waved his hand, and a new spell seized us. I have learned since that magic must be neat. It must be precise. A mage might cast a messy spell as Timor did then, in his haste. But all kinds of unfortunate consequences could arise.

This spell slapped into us where Grandfather and I crouched, clutching at one another. I suspect Timor tried to make us—the only two remaining Rats in Regis—disappear. But he failed in his wording or intent. And the spell went awry.

Perhaps he willed *no Rats*. And the spell took one logical course. For when the pain ended—and let it be known a spell so powerful does inflict pain—there were no Rats on the harbor front. Just three Men, two of us naked.

Chapter Three

Grandfather, who'd once had only three feet, now had but one. He told me later that as a Rat he'd once chewed off one of his back legs to escape a trap, leaving him with three. Now he had one foot and two arms.

Since I came to myself clutching him and we were naked, I could see his horrific injury. The stump had healed badly, seamed with scars.

The wizard—Timor—gasped and blinked at us. He had not expected this outcome. He shot another look at the townsmen, who drew ever closer, and waved his hand again. The quick pain of a small spell burst upon me and I was—clothed.

I wore Men's clothing. I was a Man, as was Grandfather, beside me. The horrible wizard had turned us into Men.

"Get up. Get up," he barked at us in a harsh undertone. "You are my assistants, understand?"

I let go of Grandfather, who looked very odd indeed. Most Men are ugly, with their pale, bloated faces and cruel eyes, looking always for an opportunity to cause harm. As a Man, Grandfather appeared less ugly than most. He had a narrow face and dark eyes set rather close together, a sharp nose and a sloping chin that did not jut out like those of most Men. His hair was gray.

I got to my hands and knees, and there I stuck. I did not know how to stand upright. Rats can rear, and do when defending themselves. But to balance there and walk? No.

The wizard hauled me up by the back of my coat. Once upright, I found I could balance there after all. He dragged Grandfather up beside me to stand on his one leg, clutching my arm.

How strange it was! Everything looked much smaller than it had moments before, and the perspective was skewed. I could see farther from me. The clothing felt odd against my skin—irritating. Restrictive.

"You are my assistants," Timor growled at us again. "Be silent."

Just to be defiant, I squeaked. He glared at me. His eyes—the one green and the other brown—made that glare seem twice as dangerous. Threatening. Colors were so much brighter than before, but scents had faded terribly.

The Men of Regis approached. Puffing in the lead was a stout fellow in a tailcoat and top hat.

Timor drew himself up and bowed. "Lord Mayor, esteemed gentlemen. You will see I have fulfilled my promise. Every rat in Regis is gone."

He gestured to the harbor. I turned appalled eyes there. Most of the Rats—all my family—had disappeared beneath the surface of the water. A few brave souls paddled on. I did not imagine they would last long.

Grief swamped me. Everyone I knew had perished. Regis had become a Rat desert. Only Grandfather, who was not even truly my grandfather, and I remained. As Men.

Clearly the wizard did not want to admit to the authorities that two Rats had survived his purge.

"Master Springerle," puffed the fellow the wizard had addressed as the Lord Mayor, "the purge was successful?"

"Of course." Timor bowed again. "Did you doubt me?"

The lord mayor gestured at us. "Who are these fellows?"

"My assistants, to be sure, Lord Mayor."

"The old man can barely stand."

"He has knowledge, Lord Mayor, and the younger man carries out his instructions."

"Ah. One can never underestimate the knowledge of an elder."

"Indeed." Timor swept an arm out toward the vast Forth. "You are satisfied with my work?"

The Men of Regis spread out along the harbor front. They peered into the water and spoke among themselves excitedly.

The lord mayor conferred with his fellow authorities. While he did so, Timor pushed me and Grandfather behind him.

The stout Man rubbed at his chin. "Master Springerle, it appears your magic was indeed effective. But the extent of its success remains to be seen."

"Whatever do you mean?" Timor's beaming smile dissolved into a frown. "You can see for yourself the excellence of my work. There are no rats left in the fair town of Regis. Thus, the plague that besets you will soon pass."

He added with emphasis, "You owe me my fee."

"Of course, of course." The Lord Mayor drew

himself up, though at his tallest Timor had a head on him. "However, I am sure you will understand if we withhold your fee just until we can be certain all the rats are gone."

"What?"

"It appears most of them, yes, have jumped voluntarily into the sea. But what if in fact there are some in hiding? Malingerers, so to speak. Rats are adept at hiding. They may well emerge later and reinfect us."

"Impossible. No rat could resist that spell." Timor narrowed an eye at me and Grandfather.

"Nevertheless, we will require proof they are all gone."

"What sort of proof?" Timor huffed, clearly growing agitated.

"Why an absence of rats, obviously. I and my fellows have conferred. We think a period of a fortnight would be fair."

"A fortnight?"

"If no rats emerge in that time, we will of course pay you in full."

Timor's pale and rather freckled skin turned pink. "That was not our bargain."

"It was, we feel, understood."

"Gentlemen." Timor took a step forward. "Do you truly wish to anger me, having seen what I can do?"

"Indeed, no."

"Those were rats that just jumped into the sea. Would you have it be your children next?"

The elder men exchanged horrified glances. "To be sure, no. But you can see our point. Your fee is high. We must make sure all the rats are gone. We feel a period of a fortnight will assure us of it. We can allow you the use of a house for that time, you and your— er—helpers."

"I will be paid!" Timor fairly trembled with rage. Having felt his magic, the hasty undisciplined nature of it, I personally would have done what he asked.

The Lord Mayor chose compromise. "Very well, we will pay you half your fee. And half in two weeks. That is fair."

"What am I to do marooned here for two weeks?"

"We have many fine taverns. Purported to be rat free." The Lord Mayor thrust out a bag that clinked of metal. Timor accepted it.

The Men of the town drew themselves up. A glance told me all of the remaining Rats had now drowned—the harbor lay empty. Despair gripped my heart.

What of us? I did not want to be a Man.

"Simon," the lord mayor called to a Man who stepped forward from the group.

"Timor Springerle, this is Simon Carp, who owns several properties in the town. He will take you to the house where you may lodge."

Simon Carp had black hair and a paunch. He did not look particularly happy with his situation.

As the townsfolk began drifting away, he said, "Master Springerle, come this way. It is not far."

"What of us?" To my own surprise I said it aloud this time. Apparently the enchantment allowed me to speak in the Man-tongue.

Timor looked at me sharply. For an instant I felt sure he would fling another spell at us, perhaps cast us into the sea after all. But too many Men yet lingered.

He could not be seen to treat an old Man so.

He snapped, "Well I suppose you had better come along."

Chapter Four

"I do not wish to be a Man." For the third or fourth time, I made the protest. "Please change us back."

So far, Timor had ignored me even though I spoke as politely as I could, still marveling over having the ability to speak words.

We had limped to the house in the wake of Timor, who in turn followed the direction of Simon Carp. The inside of the spacious house echoed, there being very little in the way of furnishings. I'd helped Grandfather to a bench, having mostly carried him along the way.

Then I stood surveying the surroundings and taking stock of myself. The perspective still seemed all wrong. I should be no taller than a skirting board, able to hide behind coal skuttles and under cupboards.

I felt horribly exposed standing there in my plain clothing, beginning to doubt who I was. A Rat no longer. Only, a Rat was what I *was*.

That pushed me to make my request the first time. "Please, Master Wizard, change us back."

Timor seemed mightily displeased with his situation, even though he'd been given that sack containing what I must believe was part of his pay.

Now wholly impatient, he turned on me. "I cannot turn you back. Stupid rat, do you not see that? If they spot so much as a single rat in this town—and that includes you—they will refuse to pay me the rest of what they owe."

"I will go and hide. I will take Grandfather."

He stared. "That is your grandfather?"

I shrugged. "He is someone's grandfather."

"You cannot hide well enough. I will have the rest of that payment, understand?"

He narrowed his eyes at us. "You will stay here in this house with me until I am paid in full."

I did not like that prospect. It must have showed.

"Would you prefer I wave my hand and do away with you and the old man—er, rat? That would be easier for me. I will do it."

I believed him. I have learned since that, like all else in life, magic has a price. I did not know then that casting another spell would have cost him, or I might have used it to my advantage.

I glanced at Grandfather Rat, who did not look well. I knew how the spell of transformation had pained me. I could barely imagine him enduring it.

I protested, just because it went hard with me to knuckle under to him, "I don't like having to stay here."

"Nor do I, but oh, well, you heard the Lord Mayor. What do you care anyway? It is not as if you have business to conduct. And is hiding in my house so much worse than hiding beneath the floor of some other building in the town? We are all prisoners until this is resolved."

I looked at Grandfather. He groaned.

The wizard leaned against a table and crossed his ankles, studying me. "I never realized rats were so concerned with one another's welfare. All for themselves I supposed, and bugger the rest."

He was not far wrong. We are born survivors, yet

we do live in loose communities and respect other members of our families.

I snapped, "Perhaps you should find out a little more before you go to murdering us."

"Ah! You are angry with me about what took place outside." He did not look particularly discomfited by it.

"Shouldn't I be? Wholesale slaughter. My Mother. All my family."

"Except Grandpa, there."

"He is not truly part of my family."

Timor cast a disparaging look at the skinny old Man who huddled on the bench, apparently barely able to follow the conversation.

"Tell me something. How were you able to withstand my spell?"

"I am not sure I understand what you mean."

"Let me ask it more simply. Why are you not in the harbor?"

Something about that question made me uneasy. I did not like him knowing too much about me. To Rats, secrets equal safety and safety equals power.

"I suppose we escaped the madness because we were at the rear of the crowd."

He quirked a brow. "The 'madness'?"

"What else would you call it? They all jumped to their deaths."

"I would call it a finely-crafted work of magic."

Sloppy, more like, though I did not say so.

"What happens to us if you will not change us back?"

"I did not say I would not change you back. Keep your mouths shut about what's going on, and I will change you back. Once the town is confirmed free of rats and I'm paid what the council owes me, I will be on my way. You may repopulate at your leisure after that."

Repopulate? Was he stupid as well as cruel? I would need a female for that. As a young male Rat I'd thought about breeding someday. Impossible, now.

"Meanwhile," he went on as if he discussed something of scant importance, "you can assist me."

"Assist you with what?"

He shrugged. "Whatever small jobs come up. I take such jobs frequently. You and the old man can play your part."

"Rat. He's an old Rat."

"Not for the duration he isn't. Get it through your heads you are men. And if you don't like it, all the more reason to fulfill your duty and keep on my good side."

"Grandfather is unwell."

"What d'you want from me? A physician?"

"No. He needs rest and food."

"Put him to bed, then. There must be beds somewhere in this barren tomb. Then report back to me."

I said nothing.

"Yes, Master Springerle," he said mockingly.

"What?"

"That is your proper response to me."

Oh. I was to be at his beck and call, was I? For days uncounted—for it is difficult for Rats to count. I mean if we discover there are three cheeses in a larder, we will remember *three* but not much beyond that.

I was marooned here as a Man and forced to obey the whims of the monster who had killed my family.

Could it get worse?

"Do you have a name?"

I blinked at him. Rats do not carry names the way Men do. That is, a Mother may call her offspring *Little One* the way I called her *Mother*.

I shook my head.

"I will call you Marquell. He can be your grandfather. Now get him out of here. I am expecting a guest."

A guest? To be sure, Rats visited one another often. I understood the concept. But how could he expect a guest when he hadn't known he would be here at this house?

"Go."

I helped Grandfather up onto his one foot. He had almost no strength, and I had to let him lean on me heavily.

"Come along."

We were looking for a bed. I did not suppose that consisted of shredded paper in a corner anymore. Most Men's bedchambers were upstairs, and a flight of stairs led up from the foyer where we were.

The stairs proved an ordeal. Grandfather, not only weak but confused, had to be helped up one step at a time.

"Where are we?" he asked in a blend of squeak and human speech.

"In a house, Grandfather."

"Are you one of my descendants?"

"No."

"Then why do you call me Grandfather?"

"Out of respect."

"What happened to us?"

I paused on the first landing and gazed into his

face. He'd retained his whiskers and they were still white, though now they looked like a Man's beard. His dark eyes darted back and forth, up and down, wild with distress.

"We've suffered a magic spell."

"Have we?"

"Don't you remember? We were running with the others—"

"The others." I felt the jolt hit his body when he recalled it. "All gone?"

"All," I confirmed bitterly.

"All dead?"

"Yes."

He began to moan, which made the climb no easier. We staggered to the first floor, and he peered back down the stairs.

"That Man—he is responsible?"

"He is."

"Let me go back. I want to bite him."

"Not yet." Later, so I hoped.

The hallway at the top of the stairs contained many doors. Following instinct, I made for one toward the back of the house.

The room, like those below, looked but half-furnished. There was a bed and a chest, and a cold fireplace.

"Listen to me." Gently, I settled Grandfather onto the edge of the bed. "I want revenge as much as you do. But if we kill him now, we'll never get back to being Rats. Give me some time. I'll settle him."

Grandfather eyed me. "You're a strong young Rat, even though you don't look it right now."

Was I strong enough to do what I must? Serve the

monster as he deserved before overwhelming him?

"I'm so tired," Grandfather lamented.

"You rest here. And leave the seeking of justice in my paws."

Chapter Five

Timor's guest proved to be a lady. I do not know how he contacted her, whether it was by magic or he went out while I was busy with Grandfather. But she arrived some short while later with great bustle and fanfare.

I had best touch here on my mental and emotional state, neither of which—as may be imagined—was good. Shock at watching everyone I knew jump off the pier and swim out to sea overwhelmed me. On top of that I felt anger and resentment and, let it be admitted, a good deal of hatred toward Timor Springerle.

I also felt fear, which is harder to confess. Rats do not like admitting fear, though we do experience it. I felt horror at finding myself a Man, and desperation, doubt, and—well, you can imagine the rest.

Grandfather soon fell asleep on the bed. I gave in to curiosity and approached the mirror that topped one of the dressers in the bedchamber.

Mirrors are magical, as every Rat knows. They multiply things like Men coming at you with a hammer. In the presence of a mirror, two of them come at you, from either side.

And a mirror can show you yourself. I'd seen myself before, both in a mirror up in our house and in a puddle. A fine-looking Rat of medium size, I had sleek fur that was nearly black and quick, dark eyes.

I still had quick, dark eyes, as I saw when I faced up to the mirror on the bureau. Most everything else had changed sickeningly.

I looked like a younger version of Grandfather. Same narrow head, lean cheeks, and long nose. My hair was the same color it had always been, nearly black, and grew back from my brow. My whiskers, also black, formed a neat little moustache with a patch on my chin.

I still looked like a Rat, only I didn't. The sight, as I say, made me feel like I'd eaten a bad bit of cheese.

My clothing, plain and brown, did nothing to improve my appearance. I unbuttoned the shirt and received the shock of discovering my body was nearly hairless though thin, whippy, and strong.

I could not exist like this, yet I did not know that I had an alternative.

Should I defy Timor? I wanted to, even as I had sought to defy the strength of his spell. I'd always had a rebellious streak, I supposed. Would that serve me well now? Timor seemed rash and unpredictable. His magic even more so. He could wave his hand and kill us. Or change us into something even worse than a Man, though I could scarcely imagine what might be worse.

I buttoned up my shirt—I had to admit my new fingers were even more clever than my old claws—and eyed Grandfather doubtfully. He slept deep. I could sneak out for a while.

No sooner had that thought come to me than I heard a bellow from below stairs. "Marquell!"

The name Timor had given me. I scented the air for magic—it had a particular odor, now well imprinted on my brain—and wondered whether I must obey.

Curiosity got me down the stairs to where an

incredible sight met my eyes. The foyer had exploded. That was, something had exploded inside the foyer. Bags, boxes, and other items were strewn everywhere across the floor and over all available surfaces. Amid it all stood a female Man.

Her clothing also looked as if a garden had exploded across it, all flowers, not real but painted on. She wore an amazing hat, also piled high with flowers, and had a round face which I later heard described as *merry*. Her hair, beneath the hat, was the color of dark honey.

Timor stood in front of her in a state of fawning delight.

She was his guest?

"Marquell," he said, barely glancing at me, "this is Mistress Elissabet. She will be staying with us while we are here. Take her luggage up to the Rose room."

I gaped. Luggage? Could these teeming heaps of items be considered such? And where exactly was the Rose room?

Timor said in a gentler voice than he used to me, "This is Marquell, my new servant. Ask him for anything."

"Servant?" She turned and looked at me, one brow raised. Dimples appeared in her plump cheeks and her eyes danced. "Why, he looks like a rat!"

Timor and I both froze. That had not taken long. Timor bent upon me a warning look as he answered her comment. "Kitten, do not be rude."

"I am so sorry." She did look contrite as she stepped forward and offered me her hand.

I stared at it. Was I meant to bite her fingers? Rats often grew acquainted by exchanging a nip.

"Forgive me, Marquell. I am afraid I too often speak what's in my mind without due consideration."

"Shake the lady's hand," Timor instructed.

I touched her fingers gingerly.

"I hope, Marquell, we will get on well."

"Mistress Elissabet is my fiancée," Timor told me.

"Yes, we will be married just as soon as Timor can provide me with a suitable abode." She glanced around the now-untidy foyer. "Better than this."

"It is a good house," I ventured. "Strong foundations, by the feel of it."

She trilled a laugh. "I daresay it won't fall down upon our heads. Ah, here is Constanze."

The outer door opened and a very small female Man came in carrying more luggage. She had pale brown hair tied back at the nape of her neck and looked near as miserable as I felt.

"Is that all of it?" Elissabet asked.

Constanze looked up. Her wide, pale-colored eyes held a cautious expression.

To say I was struck then at that moment would be a lie. Perhaps I should have been, considering what followed. But I felt only a flash of sympathy for her, as for a fellow sufferer.

It urged me to step forward and help her with the cases. As she deposited them, she mumbled, "One more load."

"Marquell, bring them in."

"Yes, Master Timor."

I went outside. The diminutive female Man did not follow me. In the street in front of the door I beheld a carriage.

Rats are afraid of such conveyances. We are struck

and killed often, either by the wheels or the horses' hooves, usually at night, when we venture out.

This carriage must have been hired, because the coachman just sat there on the box as I scrambled for the last few bags and hauled them in.

Hands were convenient appendages, I decided, as was being taller so I could reach things. There the advantages of being a Man ended.

I stood surveying the floor of the foyer, now a sea of washed-up belongings.

"Well what are you waiting for?" Timor asked. "Take everything up to the front bedroom, the rose-colored one."

And that said, Timor escorted Elissabet away into the front parlor.

I looked at Constanze, who drooped with weariness. She gazed not at me but at the stairs as if calculating how many trips it would take to transport the luggage.

"Do not worry," I told her. "I will carry it."

That made her look at me doubtfully. "Impossible. There is too much."

For an instant her lip quivered. I feared she would burst into tears.

Rats do not weep, not as such though we sob and moan. But I have seen small Men—called children—who lived in our house do so, and heard them, too.

"Do all these things belong to your mistress?" I lowered my voice that it should not carry to the parlor.

"Yes."

"What's inside all the boxes?"

"Clothing, mostly. Hats and gloves and little boots for her feet, and powder and rouge for her cheeks. That small case there…" She indicated a green box with her toe. "Those are all the jewels he has given her."

"Jewels? What are those?"

She gave me an odd look indeed. "You don't know what jewelry is?"

I shook my head.

"Fancy!" That seemed to distract her from her misery. She picked up several cases, including the green one. "Where are you from that you don't know jewels are pretty, valuable baubles?"

"It is a long story. I will tell you sometime." I might or I might not.

"Come on. We've a number of trips to make."

We had. In fact I lost count of them. The rose-colored bedchamber, at the front of the house, started out as bare as the one Grandfather and I shared, but didn't remain so for long.

Rats have great vitality. We can run before a Cat without tiring or chew through a wall all night to get to a bit of cheese. Constanze did tire before the end, so I finished up, carrying the last of the boxes by myself while she tried to make the bedchamber neat. When I went down to the foyer, I could hear Timor and Mistress Elissabet laughing and talking in the parlor. And I wondered at the ways of Men, that Mistress Elissabet sat at her leisure while Constanze labored so hard.

"This is the last of it," I told Constanze as I deposited a heavy case and a round box. She moved from box to box, opening many of them and hauling out elaborate dresses which she hung in a wardrobe.

I wanted to bid her rest, for she'd gone pale as paste, but figured it would be inappropriate.

"Thank you for your help, er—"

"Marquell," I said, supplying the name I'd been given.

"Marquell."

"Must you sort through all these things now?"

"Yes. It will take me hours."

I did not suppose I could help. I did not recognize most of the things she pulled from the cases, and my rough hands would likely tear the garments.

"Is Mistress Elissabet a good mistress?" I asked, for reasons I did not understand. Why should I care what happened to this slip of a Man? Why be concerned whether she suffered or otherwise?

Constanze paused in her labors and hissed at me, "I detest her and I would kill her, if I could."

Chapter Six

I reached the bottom of the stairs to find Timor standing with his head sticking out the parlor door, looking for me.

"Ah, Marquell, there you are. I need you to run an errand."

"A *what?*"

He ignored my bewilderment and dug into his pocket. "There is no food in the house. Go down to the shops and buy things for tea."

"Things?"

"Bread, cheese, some sweetmeats."

"Food."

"Yes, food. Nice things. Elissabet will expect that." He glared at me with his two-colored eyes as he put some coins in my hand. "Pay with this."

"Pay."

He sighed. "You trade the coins to the merchants for the food. Do not cheat me, understand? And do not steal from me. I know what your kind are like for stealing. If you steal from me," he warned in a fierce undertone, "I will cut off your paw. Right?"

"Uh—yes, Timor."

"You'll have to hurry. The shops will be closing soon." He made shooing motions with his hands before ducking back into the parlor. "Go—go."

I went out the front door and stood on the stoop,

still bewildered. A number of shops lay two streets over; I'd seen that much on our way up from the waterfront. I had no idea how to deal with a merchant. I'd filched food from them in the past, but had no other contact. I reminded myself the shopkeepers would think me a Man. I should behave accordingly.

What sort of food did Men like? Cheese, Timor had said. Everyone liked cheese. I felt hungry myself, unable to remember the last time I'd had something to eat.

Perhaps, I hoped dimly, Timor would share. Grandfather needed food too, being so weak.

Food dominated a Rat's life. It seemed no different when it came to Men.

Everything looked strange, viewed from my new height, though many Men who passed by me were taller. Even though my nose no longer served me as well as once it had, I could smell the shops before I saw them. The scent of bread in particular carries far.

Bread first, then.

I entered the shop feeling furtive and ducked my head, waiting for a broom to descend upon it. None did. A Man worked behind a long counter, serving a female Man on my side of it. There was bread everywhere. Never have I seen so much food at one time, even though there were gaps on the shelves.

The shopkeeper glanced up at me. "Be right with you, sir."

Sir? Was that an insult?

The female Man left without shying away from me and screaming as most female Men did. I took her place at the counter.

"What will it be?" The shopkeeper had gray

whiskers and fierce blue eyes which he fixed on me. I almost turned tail and ran.

"Bread."

"What kind?"

"I beg your pardon?"

"We don't have much left. I'm getting ready to close."

"Yes. I'm sorry I come so late."

He looked surprised. "That's all right. Here to serve, aren't I?"

"My master sent me for bread."

"I see. Simple, are we? Did your master say what sort of bread?"

I shook my head.

"I've got rye, pumpernickel—a nice dark loaf— and some white left. Your master, is he gentry?"

"He's Timor Springerle."

"Oh! The one who ridded us of the rats? Only the best, then." He slapped a pale loaf onto the counter. "Since it's for Master Springerle, I'll let you have two loaves for the price of one." He laid a second loaf beside the first.

"That's very kind." I was not used to Men being kind.

"That's all right."

"I must exchange these for the food." I drew my hand from my pocket with some of the metal pieces on the palm. "I do not know how much."

He plucked off a single coin. "Your master's staying at Master Carp's house two streets over, eh?"

"Yes."

"If he sends you out again, you come back here for bread, hear? I won't cheat you, at Arne Wagner's."

"Yes, thank you."

He wrapped the loaves in paper, and I picked them up. The aroma nearly overwhelmed me.

"I also need to buy cheese and sweetmeats. What are sweetmeats, please?"

He laughed. "You go to Madame Dieter's shop for the cheese. Tell her Arne Wagner sent you. For the sweetmeats, the shop is across the way, with the red-and-white awning."

"Red?"

"Yes, lad. Here." He came around the counter and pointed out the window. "And you'll want sausage."

"Will I?"

"Yes. And eggs, most likely. Go next door for those. But stir your stumps. It's growing late."

"Yes." He'd been kind. Would he be so if he knew I was a Rat, one of those he'd wanted to see killed? "Thank you?"

"On your way now."

I went, clutching the bread. At the cheese shop where the aromas nearly made me swoon, a stout female Man traded me three kinds of cheese for more of the metal discs. Cunningly, I once more used Timor's name, and she went next door and fetched the eggs for me, since she was closing.

At the last shop, an even stouter female glared at me as I stood staring in bewilderment at the wares on display. The offerings, arranged behind glass in a case, puzzled me completely.

"What do you want? I'm closing."

"My master, Timor Springerle, sent me."

"Oh?" Her expression changed. She came and leaned an elbow on the counter. "You worked for him long, then?"

"Not very long."

"Tell me about him. Is he really a wizard, as they say?"

"Oh, yes, he has strong magic."

"Did he magic them rats? I tell you, I had them in my back room something shocking. I could hear 'em scrabbling up the walls at night." She shivered.

"All gone now, I trust."

"Seem to be. So what does your fine master require?"

"I am not certain. He is entertaining, you see."

"Is he?" She looked even more interested.

"A young lady."

"Is that so! Celebrating his victory over them rats, no doubt. Tell you what, since it's for him, I'll make up an assortment for you. And since these things are nearly a day old, I'll give 'em to you at half price."

She bustled around, filling a white box with things from the case. When she finished, I held out my hand once more, and she selected coins, her fingers brushing my palm.

Touching a filthy Rat—just imagine!

I went back to the borrowed house carrying all the parcels, and took them straight to the kitchen, where I found Constanze scrubbing surfaces.

"I thought you were working upstairs," I greeted her.

"And now they want their supper, so I'm working down here. Oh, good—you got the food stuff."

I placed everything on the table, which she had just wiped. "This is what the Men gave me."

She measured the goods with a quick eye. "You've

done well. I can make something of this."

"Do you suppose there'll be any left for us? And my old Grandfather?"

"Your grandfather?"

"He's upstairs."

"Is that who I heard groaning at the back of the house? I thought the place was haunted." Quickly she took up a knife and cut a heel of bread and a slice of cheese. "Take him that."

"I cannot."

"Why? Doesn't he have any teeth?"

"He does."

"Then he can chew that heel and won't be too fussy."

"Master Timor said if I stole from him, he would magic me or cut off my p-hand."

"It's not stealing if I give it to you."

"Oh?"

"One thing Mistress Elissabet does not do, for all her sins, is starve her servants. In fact"—Constanze popped a bit of cheese into her mouth—"she feeds us well enough and confides all as she shouldn't to me."

"Yet you hate her."

"I do."

"And wish her dead."

"Yes."

I would never understand Men. I took the portion I'd been given and started away, only to have Constanze call me back. "Use the rear stairs so they know less of what we're about." She indicated a flight that led up from the corner of the kitchen.

The back stairs, as I discovered, led to a narrow door which opened directly opposite the room where

I'd left Grandfather. I ducked into the chamber, which lay dim and quiet.

At first I thought Grandfather had perished. I roused him, and he squinted at me.

"Grandfather, are you all right?"

"I don't feel well."

"Eat this."

I helped him sit up and watched, nearly salivating, as he devoured the cheese and bread.

"You rest and get stronger." I did not want him to die. If he did, I would be the only Rat left in Regis Towne.

Chapter Seven

When I went back downstairs, I found Timor waiting for me in the kitchen. Constanze carried plates and platters out to the room beyond.

Timor held out his hand. I stared at it.

"Did you spend all the money I gave you?"

"Money?"

"Those coins."

"Oh. No." I emptied my pockets of the rest. He gave me a sharp look. "You spent no more than that?"

"No, Master Timor."

"Constanze says you brought home a lot of goods. You've done very well." He took the coins from me. They clinked together, and I realized that's what must have been in the sack the Lord Mayor gave him.

I'd been spending the blood price of my own kind.

"Master Timor, if you are pleased, does that mean I will be allowed to eat?"

He gave me an odd look. "Of course you'll be allowed to eat. Ah—I see what it is." He glanced at the doorway beyond which Constanze had disappeared. "You are used to scrounging for your food. If you keep honest with me, I will not starve you. But Elissabet does not know what you and the old man are. Nor does Constanze, so keep quiet about it."

I nodded, my every thought at that moment revolving around being at liberty to eat the delectable food.

Constanze came back into the kitchen, and Timor went out.

"There's their meal laid on," she said in her soft voice. "Let's us eat. You look half starved."

She cut more bread for us, and cheese, and set two places at the table. It felt strange sitting down there, but I'd have stood on my head for such fare. At each of our places, she set one of the sweetmeats from the white box. We sat opposite one another.

"So what's your story?" she asked.

Mouth crammed full of cheese, I just shrugged. She wouldn't believe it, and besides, Timor had just told me not to reveal my true identity.

"He's never had assistants before, in any of the places we've been. All over the kingdom he's flitted, and for the past five months my lady's followed him and, of course, dragged me along."

"Of course," I managed. "Have you been with her long?"

"Since we were both children. Her family—they were a good family once—fell on hard times and lost most everything. She's looking for a wealthy husband. She won't find one, living with him."

"Oh." I did not know what to say. Constanze had been with Elissabet since they were children and yet hated her.

It was baffling.

"Timor keeps asking her to marry him and making her promises—rich ones. But it's no life, following his coattails, and no other man will look at her if she's lived with him. Ruined, I tell you."

So Timor wanted to wed Elissabet, and she wanted

a wealthy husband. Thus he sought much riches by killing the Rats of Regis.

We had died by the hundreds for a female Man's fancy.

"Where are you from?" Constanze asked, apparently having exhausted the previous subject. "The countryside somewhere?"

"No, right here in Regis." I asked, "Why would you suppose I came from anywhere else?"

"I don't know. You seem kind of—foreign. Like you don't know too much." She put out a hand and lightly touched my sleeve. "Not that I mean anything by it. I'm glad you're here."

"Are you?"

"Misery loves company, as they say." She smiled at me. It was the first time I'd seen her smile. It made her look less pinched and sickly.

"Go on, eat your sweetmeat."

"What is it?"

"A Jaffa cake. Chocolate with orange and a bit of sponge." She picked hers up. "My favorite."

The sweetmeat was very, very good. Sweet, as the name implies, and pungent. I ate mine carefully so as to enjoy every crumb.

Constanze laughed at me. "Your nose is twitching."

"Is it?"

"Yes, and it looks so funny."

I laughed too, happy to bring such merriment to her eyes.

****

I worried a bit, after I went up to our bedchamber, that Master Timor would think I'd stolen the sweetmeat and would decide to cut off my paw. I slept on the floor, it feeling more natural to me than the bed, but kept waking, imagining he stood over me with a large butcher's knife.

Would he even need a knife to punish me? He could just use his magic.

Morning duly arrived, and I had not been punished. I arose and went down to the kitchen, using the back stairs, after promising to bring Grandfather a crumb or two of breakfast if I could.

I found Constanze already at work in the kitchen, brewing tea and toasting bread. She smiled at me. "Would you mind going out back and filling the coal scuttle from the bin there? I am almost out of coal for the fire."

I did not mind.

The yard was enclosed by a stone wall, a terrible place from which to escape, and made me feel nervous. I located the bin and filled the pail, once more marveling over the cleverness of my hands and strength of my arms.

When I went back indoors, Elissabet was in the kitchen. She half sat, half leaned on the table, and was clad in a fantastical garment, all ribbons and lace.

"Good morning, Marquell," she greeted me.

"Good morning, Mistress."

I thought she might upbraid me for taking the Jaffa cake last night. Instead she smiled so two dimples appeared in her cheeks and said confidingly, "Timor is still abed. He often sleeps late, especially if he has performed a great feat of magic like yesterday's."

Constanze rolled her eyes. "Sometimes until the afternoon."

Elissabet just laughed. "I thought I'd take breakfast here with you in the kitchen. I do hate to eat alone."

Being a Rat, I did not know much about what would be considered right and proper, but this seemed—wrong to me. Unusual, at the very least.

"Yes, Mistress," I said. "Constanze, here is your coal."

"Thank you very much. Sit down. I'll dish up."

This time Constanze sat next to me and Mistress Elissabet on the other side of the table. I was given a cup of tea and a generous portion of toast and eggs. I kept my eyes on my food while I ate.

Mistress Elissabet and Constanze chattered more like friends than servant and mistress. They spoke of something called a menu and the lack of furniture in the house and garments to be mended. To be truthful, I understood very little of it.

Mistress Elissabet suddenly interrupted herself to ask me, "Marquell, do you not like your breakfast?"

"It is very, very good."

"Then why are you dividing it up and eating but part of it?"

"I hoped to take the other half up to Grandfather. He is unwell."

"Goodness! You needn't deny yourself on that account. I would never deprive an old man of his sustenance. Constanze, is there any breakfast left?"

"Yes, in the pan."

"When Marquell is finished with his breakfast, make up a plate for him to take to his grandfather."

I gazed at Mistress Elissabet in astonishment. I'd known Men all my life. That was, I'd had what might be called a passing acquaintance with them. I'd never imagined one could be so generous.

"Thank you, Mistress."

She trilled a light laugh. "You are a curious little man. Constanze, have you asked him about himself?"

"He will not say."

Still resting her gaze on me, Mistress Elissabet leaned her elbow on the table. "Tell me, Marquell, what do you know about your master?"

"He is a powerful wizard."

"Yes. As well as a rogue and a charmer. Did he pick you up during the extermination?"

"The—the killing of the Rats, you mean? Yes."

"How's that, then?" Her blue eyes sparkled with interest.

"I and Grandfather were just there—in the wrong place, at the wrong time."

"And he took advantage of you?" Mistress Elissabet sighed, and her expression changed.

"Ensnared, just like me."

I did feel caught, but I was nothing like her.

"Go take your grandfather his breakfast." Constanze had filled the plate. "When you come down, I have some shoes for you to polish. If you do not mind."

To be sure, I did not. I could not imagine how Constanze could hate a female so sympathetic and kind.

****

Grandfather felt strong enough to get up out of bed, once he'd had his breakfast. He was still confused and begging me for explanations about what had happened to us, but I did not like to burden him further with my doubts and fears, except to say I hoped Timor would eventually change us back into Rats.

"What's the point, if everyone we knew is dead?" he mourned, and I surely had no answer to that but one.

"We are still alive," I told him fiercely, "and I intend to remain so."

When I went downstairs, Constanze met me with a pile of shoes and a tin of polish. I sat on the back step to do the work, since Constanze said she could not abide the smell of the stuff, and I thought about running away.

The sun, coming over the stone wall, encouraged it. I might be able to open the door set there using my clever hands or even climb over the wall, given my increased height. I could make off for my old haunts and disappear.

But I feared Timor's magic might follow me, hunt me down, and perhaps accomplish what he'd threatened. And how could I abandon Grandfather?

When I finished polishing all the shoes, Constanze bade me take them up and place them in a row outside the bedchamber Mistress Elissabet and Timor shared. He still had not arisen, but when I left the shoes, I could hear voices from inside—the two of them talking together. Laughter and soft moans of what sounded like pleasure.

I'd no sooner descended the back stairs than Constanze came to me, her face pale and her eyes desperate.

"There are some men at the door. They say there's a report of rats in the town."

My heart leaped. Was there hope that Grandfather and I were not the only ones left alive?

"Where?"

"I do not know. You go deal with them—I have

shown them to the parlor."

"Me?" I squeaked.

"I must go rouse Master Timor."

"He is awake. I just heard them talking."

"Talking, is it?" She rolled her eyes. "Go, go."

My heart pounding double time, I went.

Chapter Eight

The two Men in the parlor looked angry, and there is nothing more dangerous than an angry Man.

Angry Men had a tendency to throw things or to swing clubs, hoes, brooms, and any other weapon to hand. In my years as a Rat I had seen many terrible things.

As I slipped into the parlor, I had to remind myself I was no longer a Rat. At least...I was, but these Men did not know it.

I recognized one of them. The Lord Mayor himself it was, with another older fellow. They did not look happy to see me. "Where is Timor Springerle?" the Lord Mayor demanded.

"Just coming, Master."

"A servant? He sends a servant to me?"

"Only to tell you he is on his way. A very busy Man is Master Springerle."

"Not too busy for what I have to impart."

"A rat!" the second Man interrupted. "At our shop. My wife saw it."

"We have a warrantee," the Lord Mayor thundered. "It did not take long, did it? No longer than one day."

The parlor door opened, and Timor came in. He looked as if he'd been put together hastily, his hair in disarray and his waistcoat askew. He wore a composed, confident expression, though his eyes darted to me for an instant before he focused on the Men.

"Ah, gentlemen. A pleasure to see you."

"Not a pleasure," the Lord Mayor roared. "I come with dire news."

"Yes?" Timor's pied eyes grew wide.

"A report of a rat being sighted."

"Impossible."

The Lord Mayor's face turned red. The Man beside him huffed, "It's so, sir! My wife saw it run under the shed at the back of our shop."

"When was this?"

"Not half an hour ago."

"Impossible," Timor said again.

"Sir—"

"Did you see this rat with your own eyes?"

"No, sir, but my wife did. Near hysterical she is."

I edged my eyes to Timor. Was a Rat sighting truly impossible? Grandfather and I had survived. Maybe others had escaped the cruel grip of the spell.

"You gave me a guarantee!" the Lord Mayor howled. "And we gave you all that money."

"Half my fee," Timor corrected.

"Nary a rat, you promised."

"We have no proof there is a rat."

"We have no proof there isn't!"

"Well, let us repair to this good merchant's shop and see. Marquell, you are with me."

"Master?"

"Come along."

I did not want to accompany him, even though I very much did want to know if anyone else had survived. Given no choice, I followed as Master Timor and the two Men went outside where a carriage waited.

I did not like riding in that carriage with the three Men. I would very much have preferred riding atop or clinging on behind. But the journey was not long. We soon drew up in a street where a throng of Men had gathered alongside a shop.

A skinny female Man holding a broom stood front and center. As soon as Timor alit, she immediately began berating him.

"A rat! Nasty and gray it was, and ran under there." She indicated a space beneath a lean-to at the back of the main dwelling. "One of the biggest I've ever seen."

The polite smile on Timor's face didn't waver. "My good woman, I'm sure you must be mistaken. All the rats are gone."

"You telling me I didn't see what I saw?"

"Master Springerle," the Lord Mayor said, "you agree that if so much as one rat is found in Regis, all payment is forfeit?"

"My good sir, there is no rat beneath that shed." Timor pointed dramatically.

"Then what did I see? Big and gray it was, and ugly as sin!"

Timor turned to me. "Marquell, get under there."

"What?" I gaped at him.

"Look and see if there's a rat."

I stood frozen while the onlookers stared avidly.

"There isn't room."

"Nonsense. You're slim and agile." Timor gave me a significant stare. In it I saw a good deal of threat and promise.

"But—"

"We need proof there's a rat or otherwise. You're the man to go look."

I wondered what he wanted from me. If there was a Rat, would he have me lie about it? He needed that money to keep Mistress Elissabet happy.

"Go on, man," the Lord Mayor gestured at me. "Take a look."

I was used to fitting into small spaces as well as dark, dirty ones, but I honestly did not know if I could fit under the lean-to. As a Rat, I was able to compress my bones and squeeze in most anywhere. This body hampered me.

Devoid of excuses, I got down on my hands and knees and peered under the structure. Too dark to see anything. I flattened my awkward body and wiggled under.

At once I felt more at home than I did out in the world. A welcome, fusty smell met my nose, along with another I did not like so well. I'd wiggled in all the way up to my toes before I realized that, yes, someone was under there with me.

I blinked rapidly as my sight adjusted to the gloom. Someone blinked back at me from a short distance. My nose told me the truth of it, catching up in my brain.

Cat. Cat!

The terror that gripped me defies description. I found myself in an enclosed space barely able to move, nose to nose with a mortal enemy.

The Cat's yellow eyes glowed in the dark. It meant to pounce. Did it know I was a Rat?

I backed up hastily and emerged, feet first, into the bright sunlight.

"Cat," I exclaimed.

"What?"

"Eh?"

"What did 'e say? Rat?"

Timor bent a stern look on me. "It's a cat, do you say, my good man?"

I nodded, fighting down my horror.

"Never!" exclaimed the merchant's wife. "I saw its fur! All gray and ratty it was."

A furor ensued. Timor interrupted it by gesturing at me. "Bring it out, Marquell,"

"What?" He could not have said what I thought.

"Get back under there and haul the cat out so we can all see it for what it is."

Send a Rat to haul out a Cat? I shook my head wildly.

"Surely you're not afraid of a mere cat?"

A mere Cat? "Master, that thing has claws. Big ones."

"Grab it by the scruff of the neck."

"There isn't room."

"There is. Go on, now."

I shook my head again. The Lord Mayor made an impatient sound, and people in the crowd began to jeer.

"He's afraid!"

"Of a cat."

"Some servant for the mighty wizard!"

Timor pointed at me, and his eyes sparked with golden light, almost making them appear the same color. I felt a jolt of magic, just the merest touch of it. Yet that was enough to get me back on my hands and knees despite my terror.

Which was worse? Facing the Cat or facing the wizard?

I shimmied under the shed. The Cat hissed at me and blinked its eyes. I froze.

How was I to grab such a beast? Its claws faced outward. It would have me before I could get close enough.

Every instinct bade me flee. I could hear those gathered outside talking and complaining. I could hear a low growl coming from the furry monster.

I tried telling myself I was a Man—many times larger than the Cat. It didn't help. I dared not touch it.

Maybe I could chase it out. "Shoo," I told the Cat. "Shoo, shoo!"

It hunkered down more ferociously. Its yellow eyes glowed in the dark.

"Marquell?" Timor called from behind.

Only one thing for it. I moved as quickly as I could and reached for the Cat. It shifted an instant before I could grab it and struck my hand, scoring the back of it with a set of razored claws.

Pain and fear went through me. I howled. The Cat yowled in return. The pain made me angry, and I seized the animal by the scruff of the neck with my other hand. I backed out at furious speed, with the Cat struggling in my grip.

Everyone exclaimed and stepped back when I emerged, butt first. I sprang to my feet and held the animal straight out while it did its best to gouge me with its back feet.

"C-cat!"

"Ah, yes!" Timor posed magnificently. "A cat, ladies and gentlemen, just as my assistant promised. And, as I promised—no rats!"

"Oh!" The merchant's wife wailed. "But I thought—from the back it looks like an enormous rat." She flushed with discomfiture.

Timor leaned toward me. "Put it down, Marquell."

"Eh?"

"Put it down."

I did, most carefully. The Cat ran away, making a path through the crowd of onlookers.

The Lord Mayor looked embarrassed. He glared at the merchant's wife and said grudgingly, "Some people need to learn the difference between a cat and a rat."

"It looked like a rat!" the merchant's wife insisted stridently.

Timor said in his best carrying voice, "Yet it was a cat. I assure you all the rats are gone." His weirdly colored eyes gleamed as he turned to me. "Is that not right, Marquell?"

I stood there, my hand dripping blood onto the ground, and said nothing.

****

We walked home, me with a cloth someone in the crowd had provided wrapped around my hand. It wasn't so far, and Timor did not speak to me. I kept silent also, until I could command my tumultuous emotions.

Then I ventured, "Master, may I ask a question?"

"Certainly."

"Why did you not just magic that Cat out of there?"

He glanced at me crosswise. "I did not think of it. I am sorry you hurt your hand. It did look well, though—you crawling out of there with that cat."

"Was it so important how things looked?"

"It will stick in their minds, that picture. They'll be less quick to call me next time. Besides, magic demands a huge effort to accomplish, and I'm still drained from the initial spell."

It had not kept him from threatening magic to compel me.

He flicked a glance at my hand. "You will heal."

I shuddered. "I hate Cats."

"Yes, you would, wouldn't you? You were very brave, considering."

His approval did nothing to gladden my mood.

"Master Timor, are all the Rats truly gone?"

"Yes indeed. All but two." He winked at me. "You saw them go into the sea, did you not?"

"Yes. But I hoped—"

"Ah, hope. The most magical elixir of them all." And he whistled a cheery tune the rest of the way home.

Chapter Nine

Back at the house, Timor explained the situation to the female Men, giving a lively demonstration of all that had transpired, and told Constanze to bandage my injured hand.

"Come into the kitchen," Constanze bade me.

I did, while Timor and Elissabet slipped into the parlor.

Constanze sat me at the table and unwrapped my hand, which still oozed blood from a row of four gouges.

"Nasty." She clucked her tongue. "Good thing it's your left."

"I favor my left p-hand." Most Rats did.

"I'll need to clean that before I bandage it up, so you don't take a fever. No telling where that cat's been."

I sat meekly while she bustled around gathering a basin of warm water, from the back of the stove, and other supplies.

"Hold tight, Marquell. I will do my best not to hurt you."

In an effort to distract myself from the procedure, I studied her. Her face hung very near mine as she bent over my hand across the table.

Most Men are ugly and terrifying. Emotions—like anger and hate—come and go so quickly in their faces.

Constanze seemed different somehow, her face very pale and weary, the bones so delicate. Strands of light brown hair had escaped confinement at the back of her neck and fluffed around her cheeks. Her eyes looked sad and serious, and her lips drooped at the corners.

"Now," she said, "you tell me your version of what happened."

"Eh?"

"I heard what Master Timor had to say. But that's what you might call the official version. He has a way of talking things up."

I told her while she cleaned and bandaged my wounds, finishing with, "He didn't care how frightened I was, going in after that beast, or whether I got hurt."

"He wouldn't, would he?" Her gray eyes met mine for an instant. "It was all about him and what kind of impression he made. Let me tell you, Marquell, it's always about *them.* Elissabet is the same way. She may come in here all charm and talk to us when the mood takes her, but don't be fooled. She would toss you under a carriage as fast as look at you."

"Is that why you hate her?"

"One of the reasons."

"She seems quite nice."

"*Seems* being the word, my lad. You just be wary they don't take advantage." She smoothed the bandaging carefully and gave me a crooked smile. "No matter. I think you were very brave."

"Do you?"

"Indeed. I like cats, me, but I wouldn't take one on when it had its claws out and was feeling trapped. That takes courage, it does."

She had no idea.

Constanze did something astonishing then. She picked up my injured hand from where it lay on the table, raised it to her lips, and touched them to the bandaging. It made for a moment, a special moment between just the two of us, and I came over all warm. Light blossomed in her gray eyes.

"There, now, there's a kiss for healing. You'll be all better soon."

That was a kiss? And it had the power to heal. Who would have guessed?

****

The next day, while helping Constanze clean some of the other rooms, I found a wooden cane, which Constanze suggested I give to Grandfather. With its help, he was able to get out of bed and even to come down to the kitchen, where he helped by snapping peas and peeling vegetables for supper.

Master Timor and Mistress Elissabet had gone out that morning. So it was just the three of us in the house, and the mood lightened. Grandfather still seemed quite bewildered by what had happened to us, but Constanze made nothing of his confused comments, seeming to chalk them up to his age and infirmity.

Timor and Elissabet arrived home at midafternoon and in great excitement.

"Make ready, Constanze," Elissabet announced, calling us to the parlor. "We have purchased a whole houseful of furniture that will soon arrive."

"But—" Constanze stared around the room. It was sparsely furnished, yes, but did contain a sofa, chairs, and several tables. "What of all this?"

"Cast it out." Elissabet waved a hand.

"It belongs to Master Carp," I protested.

"Ah, yes. Then store it in one of the rear chambers. We must make room."

The rest of our day was spent lugging furniture down the main hallway to a little-used rear parlor where we piled everything. By *we* I mean Constanze and I, for Grandfather was no use, and Elissabet merely flitted around. Timor did help me carry a few larger items but certainly did not tire himself.

The new furnishings arrived in several wagons and to great excitement. There were sofas and fine cabinets, and lamps with beaded shades, and everything else you could imagine.

Constanze took me aside. "This is madness. Do you know what all of it must have cost?"

"Timor had a sack of coins." Such did he call the metal discs.

"Even so. We are to stay here but a fortnight. How will we take all this with us when we move on?"

"Will we move on?"

"Master Timor is what's called an itinerant wizard. We always move on from job to job."

"Perhaps it will be different this time."

Mistress Elissabet was very happy—almost giddy—that evening. Timor had sent me to the shops for more groceries, and Elissabet told Constanze to prepare a variety of dishes so we could celebrate. Of course, Timor and Elissabet celebrated in the dining room while Constanze, Grandfather, and I ate in the kitchen.

After, while I helped Constanze clear the table and wash up, the two of them danced in the parlor and laughed, quite gay.

"Do you begin to see?" Constanze asked me as we

stood over a mountain of dishes. "We do all the work, and they have all the pleasure."

"Yes. But Master Timor pays for all this. The food. He earned the dwelling." By killing everyone I knew. Maybe I should hate him just as Constanze did.

"I know. But they are so selfish. And I am so tired." To my surprise two tears rolled down her cheeks.

Grandfather had already gone up to bed. I told Constanze, "Why don't you go rest? I will do the washing up."

"With your poor hand?"

"I don't mind."

"Oh, Marquell, you are so kind." Suddenly she broke down completely, weeping in earnest. She mopped at her face with her apron—to poor effect since the apron was already wet.

I turned her to face me. "Never mind all that. Go put your feet up. I can finish this work."

To my shock, she wailed harder. "That's not fair. Why is life so unfair?" And just like that, she stumbled forward into my arms.

I have said Constanze was a tiny little thing. I had not been an especially large Rat and was not particularly tall as a Man, but her face only reached my chest. Now she clutched at me and burrowed in. Even unversed as I was in the ways of female Men, I could tell she sought refuge.

"There, now." I wrapped my arms around her. "No need to weep. Life isn't fair. Not much we can do about it."

She blubbered into my shirt, "You're so good. So brave."

Was I? Rats generally accept their lot. Granted, I was being asked to accept a huge change, but she didn't know that. She couldn't suspect I grieved everyone I'd once known. "Things could be worse."

"I don't see how. But maybe you're right. It's better with you here."

"Is it?"

She stopped crying and looked up at me. "Very much so. I have someone to talk to and to—to share my misery."

"Always a fine thing."

She smiled ruefully. Light sparked in her pale eyes. "You're right, it could be worse. You might leave. Marquell, tell me you won't leave."

"I don't know how long Master Timor will keep me in his service." I hoped once he received the rest of his payment, he'd change me and Grandfather back into Rats. "It isn't up to me."

She wrapped her arms around me still more tightly. "I don't want to lose my only friend."

Nor did I. Even if she was a terrible female Man.

"Go and rest," I whispered.

"I will not. As if I would abandon you to this mess. I will wash and you may dry. We will soon have it done. And then maybe, after, you will sit outside and look at the sky with me."

"Yes, if you like."

****

Master Timor and Mistress Elissabet were still dancing when we went outside. It had just started to grow dark, and the air felt cool after the overheated kitchen.

We sat side by side on the back stoop and gazed at

the walled garden. At least, I did, until I realized Constanze looked up, instead.

"I love to look at the sky," she murmured.

"Do you?" I followed her gaze. It was a clear night, and above the lights from the town, the stars shone.

"No moon tonight. Have you ever wondered what it would be like to fly to the moon?"

I never had. "What do you think it would be like up there?"

"Cool and sweet, like spun sugar. At least, that's what I imagine. Do you know why I like to look at the sky?"

"Why?"

"Because the stars and moon I can see from here are the same as I might see anywhere in the kingdom or beyond. Looking at them makes me feel—I don't know. Free."

That sounded nice.

I confessed, "I've never looked up much. Too busy, I suppose, with getting by."

"People like us, we're expected to sacrifice our dreams to make the likes of *their* dreams come true."

"Do you have dreams, Constanze?"

"I used to."

"Tell me about them."

"Why?"

"Maybe if you do, you'll remember them, and then you'll still have them. Yes?"

"Oh, Marquell." She reached for my unbandaged hand. "You are very sweet."

I didn't think any Rat had been considered so before, by any Man. But with her eyes on the stars and her hand in mine, it didn't matter. We sat late while she spun me beautiful stories about owning a cottage in the forest, stories both of us knew would never come true.

Chapter Ten

"Oh, Marquell, it's just the most dreadful thing!" Constanze greeted me thus when I descended the back stairs to the kitchen one morning. She stood at the stove, whipping a bowl of eggs, her eyes wide and face pinched with unhappiness.

Five days had passed since we sat together in the garden, when she'd told me about her unlikely dreams. Our relationship had unquestionably changed. She seemed to rely upon me more and confided in me often; I found a measure of comfort in this. I supposed we could be considered friends.

To be sure, I'd had friends as a young Rat, mostly members of my family with whom I'd scrabbled and played follow-the-leader. This felt vastly different.

"What's happened?" I eyed her in dismay. I'd acquired the ability to tell when she truly felt upset, as opposed to when she was expressing some minor annoyance.

"They have decided to throw a grand dinner party."

No need to ask the identity of *they*. The whims of only two individuals ruled our lives. More and more, I understood why she resented them so.

"What's that, exactly?"

She poured the beaten eggs into the pan and turned to me. "I heard them talking about it—with the house all the way she wants it, she will invite a lot of people in for a fancy dinner. People of the town. She says it's to be a celebration of their betrothal. But I know the both of them just want to show off."

"Oh." I contemplated it. "And that's bad?"

"Very bad. So much work to be done in preparation—mountains of food to cook. And who do you think there is to do it all? You and me."

My heart sank. Constanze was good at sussing out the ramifications of things that happened. Far better than me.

"But—we already have as much work as we can manage." Timor set me tasks all day long, and I helped Constanze as much as I could. Our days began early and ended late. "There isn't time for more."

"I know that. But there are no excuses." She wiped a tear from her pale cheek. "We shall have to accomplish the impossible."

"When is this grand dinner to take place?"

"In two days."

"Perhaps I can speak to Timor."

She shook her head sorrowfully. "You think it would do any good?"

"Well, perhaps. I can make him see that he needs more servants, or such."

"I have asked for help before. I never got any till you came."

"After breakfast, Constanze, I will speak with him."

Breakfast went by as it always did, with Constanze, Grandfather, and myself eating in the kitchen between bouts of running everything Timor and Elissabet might need into the dining room. After, I helped Constanze clean the pots before I stepped into the parlor, where I could hear Timor and his lady talking.

"Master, might I have a word?"

Timor, wearing no coat but his embroidered waistcoat over a crisp shirt, and black trousers, lounged in a chair while Mistress Elissabet chatted at him. He looked surprised by my request.

"You wish to speak to me, Marquell?"

"Yes, Master."

He waved a hand. "Well, go ahead."

I glanced at Mistress Elissabet, thinking this would be easier without her there.

Immediately, she said, "I suppose you've heard the exciting news."

"Mistress?"

"About our dinner party. Don't worry, you shall have a new shirt and coat to wear, since you'll be serving."

Now there was an ironic thought: the grand folks of Regis Towne, who'd purchased the death of so many, being served their dinners by a Rat.

If only they knew.

But I began to see this upcoming event as Constanze did, a mountain of work.

"Master…" I switched my gaze from Elissabet's rosy, enthusiastic face to his. "Do you think it's possible for just the two of us to produce such a—a grand event?"

"Two of us?"

"Me and Constanze."

"You have your grandfather, surely."

"Yes." Even though I'd found that old walking stick in one of the rooms and given it to Grandfather, he still wasn't up to much beyond stumping about or sitting at the table and performing simple tasks. He didn't seem to have recovered completely from the effects of our transformation and frequently asked me where we were, and why.

"Master," I began again.

Elissabet said, "Go ahead, Marquell, and speak. I have told you—do not stand on ceremony with us."

"I am afraid all this will be too much for Constanze. She is already burdened with so much work—"

Elissabet shot me a knowing look. "Has she been complaining to you? Constanze always complains. It is part of her personality. But we love her anyway. Do we not, Timor?"

"Yes, my dear, of course."

"No." I struggled on. "She has not complained."

Elissabet trilled a laugh. "Miraculous!"

"It is just that I can see all she has to do and cannot imagine a party—"

"It will come together." Elissabet waved a hand airily. "It always does."

"Even so, Master, I was thinking that if perhaps you could magic some of the preparations—"

They both laughed.

Timor smiled at me, but the smile wasn't a pleasant one. "You would have me spend my magic on a dinner party? My magic, Marquell, is a precious commodity. It costs me to use, and it provides for this household. Do not be foolish."

I tasted despair then.

"That reminds me," Timor said, "I will have the invitations ready this afternoon for you to take around town and deliver. Meanwhile, you had better go as soon as the shops open and order the food. Employing no theft, mind."

Ever since that first time, he had been sending me to the shops, happy with the amount of coin I brought back to him.

"I have a list we've drawn up." He produced a narrow sheet and thrust it at me.

"Master, I cannot read."

"Oh." He looked disappointed.

Elissabet said, "Constanze can. Take her with you. There will be too much for one person to carry anyway."

Timor gave me a small pouch of coins. "Be careful, now."

I'd learned to be most careful, always.

****

"You are really very good at this," Constanze said as we struggled home many hours later, burdened with purchases. We had all we could carry. More would be delivered by the merchants. "You got some fine bargains."

"We make a good team." She had read out the list and directed me to the proper shops. I had done the bargaining.

To my surprise, she laughed. It was a weary laugh, but it pleased me all the same. "Very clever of you, playing upon Master Timor's fame the way you did and all he's done for Regis. People could not give things away fast enough."

I grimaced in return. "I know. Master is always surprised at how much coin I bring back to him."

She stopped walking and stared at me. "Is that so? And you hand it all over to him?"

"Yes."

Her pale eyes narrowed. "I am wondering if you should. If the change is more than he's expecting, you might hold back a few coins."

"But—that would be stealing."

She gazed at me steadily. "So it would."

"He told me if ever I stole from him he would do terrible things to me." I lowered my voice even though others on the street rushed past us. "Magical things."

"I am not talking about taking much. Out of all these purchases and the things yet to be delivered, he will never keep track of the cost."

"He trusts me."

"Precisely. That is why you can get away with it. Let me see that purse he gave you." She'd watched me pay out from it at shop after shop. I dug it from my pocket and handed it to her.

"Why, it is still quite plump." She put some of her packages down by her feet and opened the purse. "If one or two coins happened to disappear out of here, like this"—she extracted a few and put them in her pocket—"who's to know?"

"He might."

"He won't."

"I cannot steal from him."

"You have not. I have." Calmly, she handed the pouch back to me and picked up her burdens. She started off, and I hurried to keep up, my jaw working and no words coming.

After several moments, she shot a look at me. "Do you want to live under his thumb all your life?"

"Am I under his thumb?"

"Look at the life we lead. At their beck and call

from early to late, subject to every whim, and always tired."

What I wanted was to be turned back into a Rat. Our servitude would last only a while—at least mine would, while hers seemed endless. Meanwhile there was plenty of food to eat, more than I'd ever had, a dry place to sleep, and Constanze's company.

It wasn't so bad.

"I will put this little bit aside, Marquell, in a fund—for us. With some money, we can perhaps one day strike out on our own."

Us? Was there an us?

"You and me, you mean?"

"Why not?" She cast another look at me. "You must know I like you ever so well."

But she didn't know I was a Rat. I would have to tell her, for Timor would one day turn me back. If I proved fortunate.

I need not tell her now. I ventured a hand into my pocket and weighed the coin purse. It still felt heavy enough.

Timor would never know, would he? I'd never seen him truly angry and had no wish to.

Chapter Eleven

Mistress Elissabet expressed delight with all our purchases. When we arrived home, she followed us into the kitchen, eager to investigate them all.

"Capons! You got the capons! Excellent. And these tiny chocolate tortes. How elegant they look. Timor? Timor, come look at all this."

Master Timor soon sauntered in, his waistcoat unbuttoned and a pleasant look on his face. He stood watching while Elissabet admired everything, and I wondered if he calculated up the prices in his head. But apparently not, for when Elissabet finished and clapped her hands, he smiled.

"You've done well, Marquell. You have my purse for me?"

I handed it over, and he took it without comment, listening while Constanze spoke of all the things still to be delivered.

"Oh, Timor," Mistress Elissabet gushed, "it will be such a marvelous dinner party! Constanze, have you readied my gown? I wish to wear the primrose yellow one, mind."

Constanze, who looked exhausted and whose hair straggled from its bun, merely nodded. I put the coins out of my mind. Surely Constanze deserved them for all she did.

The next day and a half proved a whirlwind of

activity. I had of course taken all the invitations around town that very morning, and many recipients had responded on the spot. Only the best of the city would be there, so Mistress Elissabet insisted—the Lord Mayor and his lady and other important dignitaries.

I helped to clean the rooms these visitors would see. I and Grandfather helped prepare the food and set the table. I was given a new set of clothes, as I would be visible while serving. I wondered how these important Men of Regis would feel if they knew a Rat handled their plates.

"Almost ready and done." I tried to comfort Constanze on the day, as she hurried up to help Mistress Elissabet dress, leaving me in charge of the pots and ovens in the kitchen.

She looked distracted. She too had been given suitable clothing, a pretty little dress and ruffled white apron and a cap covered in lace. But her hair straggled out from beneath.

"Don't believe it," she told me. "After it's over, there'll be all the cleanup. And who, I ask, d'you think will be in charge of that, eh?"

Then, as she passed me by, she did an incredible thing—reached up and kissed me on the cheek. Light flickered in her eyes. "I don't know what I'd do without you, Marquell. And I will say, you look handsome in your livery."

She was gone before I could reply. I did not know what livery might be, but I liked the way she'd looked at me. Why would she call me handsome? I supposed I might be fine-looking as a Rat, but in my present guise? No.

Mistress Elissabet regularly laughed at my

appearance—in a kindly way, of course—calling me a funny little fellow. She'd even repeated once or twice that I looked a bit Rat-like in my features. When she did, Timor just stared at me and shook his head.

"That female Man fancies you," Grandfather pronounced unexpectedly once Constanze had gone upstairs. In truth I'd forgotten he was there beside the fire, turning the roast on its spit.

Fancied me? When a female Rat fancied a male Rat, she became receptive to his company, and he might father her next litter.

I shook my head. "You must be mistaken. We're just friendly."

He chuckled. "I don't think so."

That thought lodged in my head through all the furor that followed. Constanze eventually got Mistress Elissabet dressed. Timor, fortunately for me, dressed himself. When the guests began arriving, I was expected to greet them at the door, bow—Timor had demonstrated how, for me—and escort them to the parlor, while Constanze and Grandfather struggled on in the kitchen.

Impossible for three people, and one of them lame, to carry out all the necessary duties. Constanze seemed to be everywhere—in the parlor serving drinks, in the kitchen plating food, and running to fetch Elissabet's fan when she asked for it. I did my best to help.

Twelve guests we had, when they went in to sit at the table—that made fourteen with Elissabet and Timor. And oh, the food that was served! I had never seen the like. There was the roast, all crisped up fine, fish with capers, and tiny individual souffles over which Constanze had labored frightfully. There were truffles and spirits, and more other things than I could name. I stood by after serving each course and watched them eat—starving because it all looked and smelled so good, and I'd had nothing to eat all day—and I listened to the talk, which seemed peculiar to me.

How Men do talk! They have a way of talking about themselves, boasting without truly boasting. They refer to their importance and their accomplishments. Even the amount of coin in their pockets.

They talked about the master and mistress's betrothal, though some of the female Men seemed a bit sly about it, a thing Mistress Elissabet did not appear to notice. She took a good deal of wine—I kept refilling her glass—and laughed a lot, very bright and gay.

I had to stand there, silent, while the talk came around to the dispatch of the Rats—that's what they called it.

"Not one rat seen in all the city!" the Lord Mayor gloated, and Timor flicked a glance at me, stationed directly behind the Lord Mayor's chair. That glance contained a warning, but I did not intend to speak even though I would have liked to dump the contents of the bottle I held over the Lord Mayor's head.

After the beautiful little chocolate tortes were served, the guests repaired to the parlor, still praising the fare. I had to go with them and stand by to serve more drinks while Constanze cleared all the dishes from the table. The talk became silly. Mistress Elissabet giggled a lot, and at last I was able to show the guests out.

By then, my paws ached. I went into the kitchen to find ordered chaos. Constanze looked up wearily from a sink filled with soiled crockery.

"Are they gone, then?"

"Yes. Only Master and Mistress left in the parlor. Where's Grandfather?"

"I sent him up to bed after he ate."

"Did you eat?" I asked longingly.

"Not yet. I waited for you."

That pleased me, though I didn't understand why it should. She withdrew her hands from the suds and pulled me to the table, where we sat opposite each other.

We gorged. We ate leftover roast and capon, and spirits and all the rest of it, followed by the little tortes, which were delicious. I felt—well, happy, being there with her.

She sighed and relaxed when we were done. "Here." She smiled and nudged a second torte at me. "Have another."

"I couldn't. I'm bursting."

"I'll put it aside for you, then, for tomorrow."

Tomorrow. I felt content at the thought of it even with all the work to be done.

"Why don't you go up to bed?" she suggested.

"Are you going?"

"Not till I get most of this cleared away."

"It'll take hours. I'll stay and help you."

Tears came to her eyes. "Marquell, are you sure you're not an angel?"

"What are them?"

She laughed unsteadily. "Someone who is very, very good."

Not me, then. I was a Rat.

Mistress Elissabet put her head around the door into the kitchen while still we did the dishes, saying she and Master were going up to bed. She did not thank us for all our hard work, but she did seem pleased.

"I think our guests enjoyed themselves, don't you?"

"I think," Constanze told me after Elissabet had gone, "those fine ladies of Regis consider Elissabet no better than she should be."

"Why is that?"

"Living with Master Timor as she does without benefit of wedlock. Yes, they might be betrothed, but it's shocking."

"Is it?"

"By the standards of those ladies, yes. Not respectable, like."

"But Mistress Elissabet and Master Timor seem very happy together. Isn't that the important thing?"

"It should be."

Before we went up to our beds at last, Constanze once more kissed me on the cheek. This time she laid hold of both my forearms and we stood so for several minutes as if connected.

"Thank you, Marquell."

"For what?"

"For being here, I guess."

I wanted to think about that before I went to sleep, to contemplate the sweetness of it. But I fell into slumber as soon as I curled up in my blanket nest.

****

It seemed as if I woke only moments later. I suppose in truth I hadn't been abed long. Sunlight flooded the chamber and dust motes danced in the bright beams. The chamber seemed unnaturally quiet.

I scrambled up and looked to see if Grandfather

had risen ahead of me. He still lay in the bed, but I knew at once something was not right.

Usually he slept on his back, his mouth open and the air seething in and out. Now he lay on his side, his hands raised—like claws—and face frozen in a rictus.

Despite this it took me several moments to realize he was dead. Passed at some time during the night. Had he already been gone when I came up to bed? I hadn't lit the lamp then.

He felt stiff and cold. I stood beside the bed, staring at him, grieving that he should have died in this, a foreign form. Realizing I was the last remaining Rat in all of Regis Towne.

Chapter Twelve

"They killed him," Constanze declared indignantly when I went down to the kitchen and told her. "With their hard work, they did."

After looking into my shocked face, she pulled me into her arms. "Cry if you want to."

"Should I cry?" I asked, half muffled by her cap.

"He was your grandfather. You were fond of him."

I was. I didn't weep, but my nose twitched violently. It felt nice having her arms around me, her hand stroking my hair.

Eventually she released me, though she kept hold of my hands.

"He was very old," I ventured. "Gray-furred. Perhaps he did not die from the work."

"Gray-haired, you mean. Well, but for the past three days he had no rest. Marquell, I am sorry for your loss."

I nodded. "What's to do?"

"You'll have to tell Timor. If he has any decency in him, he'll pay for a funeral."

"Funeral?"

"A burial, Marquell."

"Oh." Rats were seldom buried. Usually we crawled away somewhere private to die and decomposed there. Of course, all the Rats who'd jumped into the Forth lay at its bottom.

I supposed I could not leave Grandfather where he was in the bed.

"All right. I will tell Timor."

"He's not up yet. Neither of them is. Goodness, I suppose I'll have to make breakfast for one less! It will take some getting used to." She shot me a serious look. "It's just the two of us now, Marquell, against the world."

I liked that idea.

When Timor arose, much later in the afternoon, I told him the news. He was alone in the parlor. Mistress Elissabet was still primping, upstairs.

He gave me a stare. "Well! I suppose that's one fewer for me to worry about."

"Master?"

"One fewer rat," he clarified. "Now it's just you who can tell on me."

It sounded like he was glad Grandfather had died. "Grandfather was trustworthy," I protested.

"He was old and confused. He might have said anything." Timor gave me a fierce look. "You won't tell. You know better."

"Constanze told me to ask you about—about, well, what to do with his body."

"Constanze did, eh? You and Constanze seem to be getting very friendly."

Something in the sharpness of his gaze told me he did not particularly like that idea.

"We are thrown together very often," I said plaintively, keeping from him how I truly felt about Constanze.

And how did I feel about her?

"You'll want to be careful," he warned. "Constanze

is a sharp one. And as Elissabet keeps saying, you look quite ratty still. Constanze just might tumble to what you are."

Was looking Ratty truly so terrible? Constanze did not seem to mind.

"I will be careful," I assured Timor. "What should we do with Grandfather?"

"Let me make some inquiries. There is probably a paupers' graveyard somewhere in the town."

"Paupers?"

"People who are penniless. You can't pay to bury him, can you?"

I shook my head. "Constanze said you might see fit—"

"He's a rat, when all's said and done."

I returned to the kitchen, where Constanze took one look at my face and asked, "What did he say?"

"He will ask about a pauper's grave."

"Come, I'll go up and help you with him. Let me fetch a sheet."

I was half afraid I'd return to the bedchamber and find that Grandfather had turned back into a Rat. But I found him just as I'd left him. Apparently even death could not alter Timor's spell.

In the end, Constanze helped me wrap him in the sheet from the bed, very kindly folding his arms across his breast first. We left him bundled in the bedchamber, and she made me a cup of tea in the kitchen.

Soon Timor looked into the room. "There's a man here with a cart to take your grandfather away. Best bring the old—er—man down."

Constance faced off with Timor. "He'll never carry his grandfather by himself."

Timor called the Man with the cart inside to help me. We carried Grandfather down the back stairs and laid him carefully in the rear of the open wagon. I asked the Man, "Where will you take him?"

"Paupers' field. Want to come? They've got the hole open, and we'll just drop him in."

I shuddered. "No, thank you."

"Suit yourself, friend."

The cart trundled off and left me wondering. Was that truly a better fate than resting at the bottom of the sea?

****

Grandfather's death changed little. I missed him, of course, but he'd never said much, and his words were often confused. I moved to the bed for sleep and picked up the few duties he had performed. The biggest change was my knowledge that I was now the very last Rat in Regis Towne.

The days sped by, and the end of the fortnight quickly approached. No other Rat sightings had been reported. Despite the fact that Constanze insisted the women of the town secretly sneered at Elissabet, the Mistress had ladies in for tea. I think she enjoyed dressing up in her most elaborate gowns and playing hostess, even though it ran Constanze off her feet.

Master Timor sometimes went out to take small jobs of magic on the side. He always came back with a satisfied look on his face and money in his pocket.

One day when Mistress Elissabet had some ladies in, I overheard what I shouldn't. It being a cold, rainy day, I carried some firewood into the parlor where the guests drank their tea, as Constance had asked me. I'd left one load and decided another armful would be a good idea, when I heard the ladies talking.

About me.

"La, Elissabet!" one of them said in her high, clipped voice. "You have an odd-looking servant."

"Marquell, do you mean?" Elissabet asked.

"That creature who just brought in the firewood. However did you come by him?"

I froze outside the parlor door where I stood. What would Elissabet say? She didn't know the truth about me.

"I don't know. Timor picked him up somewhere. His people must be from foreign parts."

"That might explain it. He looks like he was starved in his youth. And that nose!"

Elissabet tittered. "I always think he looks a bit like a rat."

They all laughed then. Laughed at me.

"Ooh, no, not one of those vile creatures!" a lady quipped. "I'm so glad they are all gone."

I tiptoed away then, under cover of their laughter.

"What is it?" Constanze asked when I entered the warm kitchen. Constanze had a stew on for supper. "I thought you were taking those logs to the parlor."

"I did. I cannot."

She tipped her head at me. "Eh? What's the matter? You look strange."

"I know I do. That's the trouble, isn't it?"

I put the logs in the kitchen woodbox and shed my jacket.

"Come sit at the table with me." Constanze invited. "Before she rings for me again."

I did as bidden. She took my hands in hers. "What is it, Marquell?"

"Am I ugly, Constanze?"

"Ugly? You? No. What have you heard?"

Timor was right about Constanze; she was quick. "The ladies were talking about me. About my appearance."

"I see."

"They were laughing."

"Curse those uppity snobs." Constanze bit her lips. "Here, you listen to me. You might look a little different from other folks. That sharp nose and all. But I don't think you're ugly, not at all. It's—exotic, yes, that's the proper term. These ladies with their bloated, overfed husbands just can't appreciate a fellow like you."

"Do you think that's it?" Or it might be that I was a Rat.

Suddenly I wanted to tell her, wanted to unburden myself and share this most terrible secret. But quite apart from the restrictions Timor had laid upon me, I liked the way Constanze looked at me. I enjoyed—and maybe needed—the warmth we shared.

How could that help but change if she found out I was a Rat? Females—as just overheard—detest my kind.

"Don't worry about those uppity women. I like the way you look very much."

I couldn't help but smile at her. "You do? That's all that matters, then."

She leaned across the table and kissed me—not on the hand or on the cheek this time but on the lips. Strange and powerful feelings poured through me. Shocked, we stared into one another's eyes.

"Marquell," she whispered, "surely you must

realize how I feel about you?"

I shook my head.

"I've never known anyone like you."

There was no one like me.

"And I—I just don't know what I'd do without you now."

All that would change, I thought again, if she found out I was a Rat. I couldn't tell her, even though the desire burned through me.

I wanted Constanze to know the truth and like me anyway.

But there was no point, was there? The fortnight and our time together would soon end.

Still holding her hands, I whispered, "When Timor and Elissabet leave here, I do not think he means to take me along."

"What?" Her fingers tightened on mine. "What makes you say that?"

"When he—when he took me on, he said it was just temporary. That he'd let me go once the fortnight here was up."

"That's dreadful!" Her eyes grew round. "I'm sure he'd take you if you ask him. Or"—she read my expression—"don't you want to come along?"

"I was born here, in Regis Towne. I've lived here all my life. I don't know how to leave."

"It's all right. You'll learn. I once had a place I belonged, and I've learned to live away from it."

But she wasn't happy. I did not say that, since she tried to help me.

"This dirty, funny town is in my blood. In my guts."

"It's a hard kind of place. Full of snobby people.

And oh, Marquell—I can't say how I'd miss you."

"I would miss you too." She had been a near-constant presence in my days. An ear that would listen. Always welcoming and kind. Constanze might be harsh with others, but never with me.

"Tell me about the place you used to live," I bade her. "You were a child with Elissabet?"

"We grew up together, yes. But we were—never the same, see."

"Of different classes?" She'd taught me about the differences in rank and perceived worth.

"Something like that," she answered vaguely. "We lived in the forest. My favorite place in all the world. Oh, how I would love to return there some day."

Then she should understand why I did not want to leave Regis.

"Marquell, I have an idea." She lowered her voice. "It's a mad idea, but sometimes those are the best kind."

"Are they?" My cousin and I once followed a mad idea and ran into a larder after some cheese. We'd been shut in and nearly died when the cook found us.

"You know those coins you gave me? The leftover ones? I have a stash. I've been saving since before you came, for enough to light out on my own. Escape this servitude and—and go home. My real home, I mean."

"How will you escape?" Timor did not keep a close eye on us. He sent us out on errands. But I always had the feeling he knew things.

Maybe not, though. He did not know about the coins.

"I've been saving and saving, and have the money hidden in an old stocking. Not quite enough yet. But how much faster it will go if you agree to help me, if we keep borrowing a little bit from what Timor gives you."

Borrowing.

"And then, when we have enough, we can find a little cottage in the woods together." Her pale cheek flushed. "Get married, perhaps."

Married? She for certain would not want that if she knew I was not a Man.

I must tell her. She was my friend—possibly a mate—and she deserved the truth from me.

I really should tell her but, I decided, gazing into her beautiful eyes, not just yet.

That night when I went up to bed, I put the lamp on the dresser and looked at myself in the mirror there. Mirrors still made me feel very odd, and I wondered how to know if what I saw on the surface was the same as what everybody else saw when they looked at me.

What was real? What illusion?

There were mirrors in the parlor, and I'd seen Constanze's image reflected there while she was dusting. It looked the same, almost, as she did to my eye.

Small. Impossibly fragile, for the amount of work she did.

So what I saw reflected now must be me.

My black hair had grown and nearly reached my collar. My dark eyes looked wary. I looked nothing like other Men.

Did I want to go back to being a Rat? Did I, if it meant parting from Constanze?

Chapter Thirteen

"Marquell, a word with you, if you please."
Mistress Elissabet summoned me into the parlor with a
wave of her hand. It was late morning, and Master
Timor had not yet arisen. I'd only just taken up his hot
water and clean towel so he could shave.

The parlor looked very pleasant with all the new
furnishings and the sunlight pouring in. The days had
begun to cool. Soon it would be autumn and then bleak
winter.

I had thought about that much. If I stayed in Regis,
I would be a Rat alone trying to survive the winter.

Elissabet seated herself on the settee and waved me
to a chair.

"You know, Marquell, I seldom stand on ceremony
with you and often come to the kitchen to talk with you
and Constanze."

Yes, usually when she wanted something.

"It is a peculiarity about me that I usually treat my
servants as friends."

"Yes, Mistress."

She gave a pout. "Perhaps that is my failing. I have
neglected to keep a proper boundary. Perhaps," she
waved her hand again, "I do not completely understand
where boundaries lie. As a result, Constanze has this
morning given me a dressing down."

I stared in surprise. She looked fully dressed up, to

me. "Mistress?"

"She says you heard me and the ladies laughing at you, and it hurt your feelings. She claims I owe you an apology."

"Oh, no, Mistress." I wished Constanze had held her tongue.

"She insists we were rude about your appearance and you were quite bothered by it. You have to understand, Marquell, fine ladies such as we take amusement in all kinds of things such as your appearance. No harm was meant by it."

That struck me like a rap upside the head. "Is my appearance truly so amusing?"

"Well—" Her lips twitched, and her eyes danced. "You must admit you have a—er—foreign look about you."

"Yes, Mistress."

"But Marquell, I'm sorry you overheard that. I had no intention for you to do so."

She was sorry I'd overheard it, not that she'd made fun of me.

"It doesn't matter, Mistress."

"It seems it does. Constanze can get quite an attitude when she is displeased and can come over all prickly. Now you may run back to the kitchen and tell her I apologized very prettily."

I got to my feet. "Yes, Mistress."

"And perhaps have an extra sweetmeat tonight after supper, to make up for it."

I did not need to tell her Constanze routinely gave me as many sweetmeats as I wanted. I did enjoy the chocolate ones.

"Thank you, Mistress."

"There, now. Run on your way."

I marveled as I went to the kitchen how little Elissabet and Timor knew about what Constanze and I did. Perhaps Timor did not use magic to watch us after all.

It might be possible to sneak a coin away, here or there.

"Well?" Constanze greeted me in the kitchen. "What did she want?"

"To apologize."

"Ha!" Constanze snorted. "And so she should. I hope you feel better."

"I do not."

Constanze lifted an eyebrow.

"I do not think she meant it," I explained.

"Quite likely not. I have had more insincere apologies from that woman than I could shake a stick at." A hard look came to Constanze's face. "There's some things an apology just doesn't make up for."

Like driving all of one's family to their death and then expecting one to provide cheerful service. But I did not say that.

"Still, you deserved an apology, and I'm glad you've had one. Come have your tea."

"What can I do to help you this morning?" Perhaps if I thought of it as helping Constanze rather than serving Timor, it would not sting so much.

Her gaze softened. "Just you being here helps me, Marquell."

And that meant everything.

****

The days counted down swiftly now. A fortnight, as Constanze had explained to me, meant fourteen days.

A week was seven days, and the fortnight was made up of two of those.

Rats cannot count, not precisely. But I found a bit of a stick in the yard early on and made notches in it for every day that passed. Most evenings or mornings I carved them.

When Constanze said we were only three marks short of fourteen, I knew I had to make a decision.

Timor and Elissabet showed no signs of packing up in preparation to moving on. They now had a home full of furnishings they would either have to take with them or sell. I knew Constanze would be given orders to pack up if it came to that, and she hadn't been, as yet.

The master continued to go out on wizarding jobs. Sometimes he took me with him. He would perform all kinds of spells from magical cleansings to banishments of evil dreams. We went everywhere, and I saw parts of the city I never knew existed. He was always treated respectfully and paid well.

We never saw a hint or caught a scent of a Rat.

One day, we traveled outside the walls of the city to the countryside. We went in a hired carriage to a lodge belonging to a landowner of some means.

He insisted the place had a curse on it and requested Timor should lift it. That is not important. The fact is I had never before been in the forest, had never been outside the hard stone and timber confines of the town.

A different world, it was. Quiet, with no rush of carriages and wagons, drays and horse hoofbeats in the background. No voices except ours—the landowner, Timor, and me—though I didn't speak—and the old couple who lived in the lodge.

"I think we've been spelled by fairies," said the old Man.

"What makes you suppose that?" Timor asked.

"I've been a woodcutter all my life. They're angry at me taking the trees, more and more of them in their grove. You know what they fairies can be like."

"I do," Timor said thoughtfully. "They can cause a right problem. I will raise wards on the lodge, against them."

The raising of wards was a complicated procedure and took some time. I didn't mind standing by. My mind was full of Constanze, for this—the forest—was the place of her dreams and longings.

Standing there patiently while Timor wove his spells, I thought I could guess why. The silence was a balm to the senses. Small, colorful birds darted among the branches of the trees, and the trees themselves— they were like living versions of the pillars I'd glimpsed in some of the great buildings back in Regis.

How I wished Constanze could have come along, for her to have a chance to experience this along with me.

Perhaps it could have eased her, provided relief from her constant unhappiness, for a time.

On the way home, as Timor and I returned to the city alone—the landowner still having business on his estate—I ventured to say, "Master Timor, I have only three days left to my sentence."

"Eh? What's that?" Timor seemed distracted.

"Three days till the fortnight is over and you turn me back into a—"

"Hush. Keep your voice down. The coachman has ears."

My voice was already down, but I nodded.

"Is that still what you want?" I'd succeeded in capturing his attention. He bent a hard look on me.

"Yes, Master."

"Only I thought you had settled in with us. I wondered if you might wish to remain a part of our household, like Constanze."

"You mean travel with you, like?"

He made a face. "As for that—the matter is not decided. It seems Elissabet likes it here in Regis. She likes having a circle of friends. We may stay a while longer."

A panicked feeling surged through me. "That does not change our agreement. No Rat has been seen. You will be paid—"

"Just so."

I whispered it. "You promised to free me. From this." I gestured to myself.

"Did I?"

"Yes, Timor."

"Hmm. I suppose it's your choice. But you might rather wish to remain as you are. You make a decent servant. And returned to your old life, you realize you'd be all alone?"

"Yes." I would have to sacrifice a lot, not least of all Constanze's company, which had become dear to me. But did he truly think I would prefer a life of servitude to freedom?

That I'd choose to remain near the Man who'd murdered everyone I knew?

"Well," he said airily, "you have three days, as you say, to make up your mind."

"Yes, Master."

"Once I'm paid the balance of my fee, you can give me your decision then."

I did not know what to say to Constanze when I got home. For days, she'd been talking about packing up the household and speculating over what Timor would do with all the new possessions. She seemed restless, as if she did want to move on.

Constanze greeted me with a smile when I came into the kitchen—not one of her strained quirks of the lips but a genuine smile that lit her eyes.

"There you are. Gone a long while, you were."

"We rode out of the city to the forest. I've never been outside the city before."

"Ah!" She froze in the act of stirring a bowl of cake batter and stared at me. "Did you so? And what did you think of it? Wait, I'll get you a cup of tea, and you can tell me."

We sat at the table together, after she brought me tea and a biscuit. I thought how comfortable this was, the two of us at ease in one another's company.

"I can see why you like it in among the trees," I said. "It's peaceful, not like here at all."

"It is magical." Her eyes sparkled. "I feel like I can breathe there, not but I do see enough of magic here," she added wryly. "It's a different sort of magic, see."

I did see. "There were birds darting about everywhere, singing. And it was as if the trees spoke to one another."

"So they do. Ah, how I'd like to hear that again, if only for a short while. When we travel, Timor, Elissabet, and I, we sometimes pass through patches of woodland, but we never linger long enough to—to—"

"Feel it?" I suggested.

"Yes." She reached across the table and touched my hand, the one scarred by the Cat. "You understand me, Marquell, like no one I've ever known."

"Constanze, on the way home, Timor shared something with me that I think you need to know. Once he is paid the balance of his fee, he is thinking of staying on here in Regis."

"What?" She looked astonished. "But he never settles."

"He says Elissabet wants to stay. She likes this house."

"And all her fine possessions, no doubt. Gracious! I did wonder how he might pry her away. But how odd it would be, staying in one place for more than a week or two."

I had always stayed in the same place, more or less. I shrugged.

"How will he earn a living?"

"I suppose he thinks there are jobs enough here in Regis."

"Or he might travel off on his own, leaving her here, once they are married. Oh, goodness, can you imagine the preparations for a wedding?" Her fingers tightened on mine. "Thank heaven I have you, Marquell. Otherwise I do not think I could manage it."

I said nothing. But my heart—yes, my heart spoke to me.

Chapter Fourteen

Timor and Elissabet stayed up late in the parlor that night, talking long after Constanze and I had gone to our beds. This was not unusual. They loved to stay up till the wee hours and sleep in the next day.

What was unusual, though, was that Elissabet came to the kitchen early that next morning, her curls still tumbled from sleep and her eyes bright.

"My dears, I have news." She only called us her dears when she was in a particularly good mood. Or when she was excited about some upcoming event.

A guarded expression slid over Constanze's face.

Elissabet perched on the edge of the big table where Constanze sliced bread for toast, and said confidingly, "I managed to persuade Timor last night."

So that's what she'd been doing when they spoke in the parlor, persuading him. But of what?

Her eyes sparkled when she asked, "What would you two dears say if I told you we would stay here in Regis a while, perhaps all winter?"

Fortunately, I had prepared Constanze for this. She shot me one look before she said, "That's decided, is it?"

"Yes. And there's going to be a wedding! Right here in the house. Can you imagine anything more delightful?"

Constanze still had hold of the knife with which

she'd been cutting the bread. She shifted her fingers on the handle, and for a moment I pictured her plunging the blade into Mistress Elissabet's breast.

In an effort to forestall this, I spoke quickly. "Exciting, indeed."

"We still have to work out all the details, of course. But I want you two to know, you are both very important to the success of upcoming events."

We would, in fact, make those events happen, for the most part.

"I hope that for an occasion of this size you're planning to take on more staff," Constanze said. "A wedding—"

"Oh, of course." Elissabet waved a hand airily. "We will hire waiters and such for the day. You two could not be expected to serve so many. Or—I know!" She clapped her hands and shot a look at Constanze. "Perhaps Timor can magic some decorations. Wouldn't that be marvelous?"

Constanze's face went white, and her hands began to tremble. I'd never seen her look that way.

Swiftly I ventured, "And surely, Mistress, some staff to help with all the preparations. The food, the setting-up. There will be so much to do."

"Oh, I am certain the two of you will be able to handle it. You are so clever. I said to Timor last night I could not imagine two better helpers."

She sincerely meant it as a compliment. I could see that. But Constanze's face had now gone the color of bone, and her eyes glittered dangerously.

"You expect," she said in a thin voice, glaring at Elissabet, "you expect us to put on your wedding? Endless days of work? Run off our feet and worn to a thread, all for your pleasure? All for no pay?"

Elissabet looked shocked. She slid down off the table and stared back at Constanze. "Well! I did not look at it like that."

Constanze set the knife on the table, much to my relief. "Perhaps you should. Who makes everything happen around here? Who prepares the food you eat? Who polishes your shoes?"

This confrontation, I knew, had been a long time coming. It had simmered in Constanze's resentment only to boil up now.

"You are like family to me, Constanze. You are all the family I have left."

"I am not your family!" Constanze drew herself up. "I am a servant. Forced to come along with you on this mad tour of the kingdom."

"I thought it a fantastical opportunity for you. We have always been together—"

"For which I have paid a cruel price."

"I have paid also!" Tears sparkled in Elissabet's eyes. "I gave up everything to be with Timor. Everything except you."

"And you were free to make that choice, as I was not." Constanze sounded unflinching. Elissabet recoiled slightly, wrapping her arms around herself. Had she truly never sensed the anger that lay just beneath Constanze's composure? They were together every day. Constanze dressed the woman and saw to her every need. Was she so self-occupied she could see no one's unhappiness but her own?

"I thought—" Elissabet half wept now. "—I thought you liked being with me."

Constanze narrowed her eyes and leaned toward

her mistress. Fiercely, she said, "You thought wrong."

They had both forgotten I was in the room by then, and I drew no attention to myself, not wanting to remind them I witnessed this terrible thing, the breaking of the fragile bonds that bound them to one another.

For they were bound—if not as Elissabet imagined by friendship, then by familiarity.

"You have spoiled my happy news!" Elissabet wailed and ran from the room.

Constanze wept too, hard, unforgiving tears that fair wracked her once Elissabet had gone. She clenched her hands into fists and stood with them pressed to her lips.

"She deserved that," Constanze declared. "She did."

Perhaps so, but it had been difficult to watch.

"So selfish she is," Constanze said to me, apparently realizing I stood there after all. "And always has been. It is all about what she wants. She wanted Timor and she would have him—follow him even though it wrecked both our lives. Well, she has him now. She won't have my soul as well."

I did not know what to say. I took her in my arms and felt the rigid distress in her muscles relax a bit. She sheltered against me, but not for long. She soon drew away and sighed.

"Do not worry," I whispered then. "I will help as I can. Let me serve the breakfast."

But nobody came to the dining room, and Constanze and I choked down our portions in the kitchen, with no enjoyment.

****

Timor came to me later, while I sat in the yard

polishing his boots. I did not know where Constanze was—busy somewhere in the house—and I had not seen Elissabet since their confrontation.

Timor looked grim. He stepped out into the dull sunlight that suffused the yard and said, "A word, Marquell."

I got up from the stoop where I sat. "Yes, Master Timor."

"Elissabet is distraught. I do not know what Constanze said to her this morning, but it has ruined her enjoyment of our upcoming wedding. Do you know what took place between them?"

"Yes, Master Timor."

"You were there?"

I nodded.

"Well, then, tell me."

Carefully I ventured, "Constanze became upset at the prospect of putting on a wedding. She feels Mistress Elissabet takes for granted all the hard work she extends in her service."

"She feels! How about what my lady Elissabet feels?"

I said nothing.

"Look, Marquell, can I speak to you man to man?"

"Man to Rat," I said.

"Ah—well it is of that I wish to speak. I know there are but a couple of days left before I get paid and our agreement, in essence, concludes. But the upcoming marriage and our decision to remain here in Regis Towne for a time changes things."

"If you are afraid someone will see me as a Rat after you change me back, I will hide." Trust me, after this, no one would glimpse hide nor hair of me.

He looked even more miserable. "I need you to stay. As a man. For just a short while—until we get through this wedding, at least."

He needed. I stared at him mutely, thinking I understood at that moment exactly how Constanze felt. He cared only about his and Elissabet's needs.

What of mine?

"We have an agreement."

"I know. But a few weeks one way or the other won't make that much difference to you. You like it here, don't you? Plenty of food, a warm bed to sleep in, and nobody chasing you with a broom."

Was that his attempt to be funny? I found none of this amusing.

"Wouldn't you rather," he wheedled, "be a man than a rat?"

"No."

"Ah, Marquell, but I need you. Look at it from my point of view. If I do not keep Elissabet happy, she will leave me. Go back to her family, perhaps."

I shrugged, and he blinked furiously.

"You expect me to believe you don't care? Ours is one of the great love stories. We are destined, Elissabet and I, to be together."

And you made me a promise.

Aloud I said, "Surely, Master Timor, if you are destined to be together, Mistress Elissabet will stay with you no matter what."

"Women are different from us, Marquell. They are far flightier. I need her. I need to give her this wedding she desires and a home here, at least for a while, in order to keep her."

"I need to be a Rat again," I told him stubbornly.

"No, you don't. At least not right away. You've been fine here all this while."

"Why do you not hire a bunch of servants? Once you are paid, you will be a wealthy man."

"I can do that, and I will. Elissabet and I have already talked about it. They will not be trained, and I cannot rely upon them as I do you, you and Constanze. Someone needs to be in charge of those I hire. Tell you what. If I elevate you, give you a new title, will that persuade you to stay? You are so good at organizing things, like the food and the seating—"

A title meant little to me, but the wheels in my head started to turn. "What about Constanze? Can she be elevated also?"

His eyes narrowed. "I begin to see that Constanze is important to you." Before I could say anything, he hurried on. "Yes, we can give her a title, something grand. How about Housekeeper?"

I wrinkled my nose.

"Madame Housekeeper?"

Would Constanze like that?

"And you can be Steward of the House, with a grand new set of clothes. How does that sound?"

I did not care about the clothes, and I scarcely understood why he found it important that I stay. But I might win something out of this.

"We can perhaps make a new bargain, Master Timor."

His gaze hardened. "What do you want?"

"I want to be assured Constanze will get the help she needs, especially for the wedding. And I ask that she should have some time off, at least part of a day, and that we have the use of a hired cab."

"A coach? You want to travel far?" He blinked again.

"I thought…outside the city. Yes."

"What do I get in return?"

"I will remain in your service until after the wedding. But once you and Mistress Elissabet are married, I may request to be changed back into a Rat at any time."

He considered it, not looking particularly happy. "And no complaining the while?" he stipulated.

I never complained, and I could not assure Constanze's compliance, but I nodded.

"Very well, shake on it." He held out his hand and gave an ironic smile. "Give me your paw on it, that is."

We shook, me thinking it would not kill me to stay a while. And my presence might do Constanze some good. How could I abandon her now?

Chapter Fifteen

Constanze was not particularly impressed when she heard her new title, Madame Housekeeper, but she was intrigued when I told her the rest of the news.

"Tomorrow is Sunday, and we have been given the afternoon off."

"What? Both of us?"

"Both of us, yes. And I am taking you out."

That made her stop what she was doing, making biscuits for dinner, and stare at me. "Out? Us?"

"A carriage will be coming, and we have leave to use it."

"You don't say!"

"I do."

"Where will we go?"

I refused to tell her, though she did her best to tease it out of me. She asked many times and went at it from several angles.

"What will we need to take with us?"

"Bring your cloak and perhaps pack a basket of food. Some of those biscuits would be nice."

Though not impressed with her new title—which she said should be Madame Drudge—she did like mine.

"Master Steward of the House!" she repeated, and her gaze warmed. "You deserve that, you do."

"Master Timor has promised to hire a large staff for the wedding."

"It will still be a terrible amount of work."

"Perhaps I can persuade him to keep one or two helpers on afterward, just so your lot is not so hard." If I could improve things for her before I left, all the better.

She laid her floury hand against my cheek. "You are so sweet to me. What would I do without you, Marquell?"

Relations between Constanze and Elissabet remained strained. Elissabet no longer came to the kitchen to make enthusiastic confidences, and though Constanze still went upstairs to tend her mistress, she returned stark and pale. Tension abounded, and I was more than glad when Sunday afternoon arrived.

The coach turned up just as Timor had promised. Carrying the basket Constanze had packed, I handed her into it as if she were royalty before stepping up to give the coachman instructions, soft enough so she would not hear.

"Where are we going?" she asked again when I joined her inside.

"You will see. It is to be a surprise." One I hoped she'd enjoy.

She looked nervous, so I took her hand. "Trust me."

"Oh, I do, Marquell."

"This is your chance to relax."

She nodded, and some of the tension went out of her.

It wasn't far to Birk's Wood, the forested area where I'd accompanied Timor to perform his magical work. The powers that be had granted us a beautiful day for early autumn, with warm sunshine and skies of deep blue.

When we entered the wood, the coach turning down a side road, Constanze leaned forward and peered through the window. She shot me a look, and her fingers squeezed mine painfully tight.

"Oh! What is this place?"

"It's called Birk's Wood. I came here with Timor the other day and, well, I wanted to bring you."

She gasped. "Why?"

"You are always speaking of how happy you were when you lived in the forest, as a girl."

"Oh, Marquell! Are we stopping here?"

"For the afternoon. I thought we could walk and have our supper and—and perhaps the quiet would do you good."

When she looked at me again, tears filled her eyes. "I would like that. I would like that very much."

The coach pulled into the yard of a cottage I'd seen when I came before—abandoned, with the roof fallen in. We would bother no one here.

The coachman came around and opened the door for us. I leaped out and handed Constanze down.

"Please be at your leisure while you wait," I told the coachman.

"I will. I brought a bit o' supper my wife put by for me, and I just may nod off to sleep. Lovely day for it."

When I turned back to Constanze, she stood staring up at the trees that surrounded the place, turning in a slow circle to survey them all. Her eyes had gone wide. They looked like moons reflecting everything around her. Never had she looked so beautiful.

"Oh, Marquell!"

"Happy?" I asked and took her hand. I picked up the basket and said, "Let us walk till we find a pretty

107

place."

So we did. Constanze kept silent, as she so often did at home, but it was a different sort of silence. Her gaze moved everywhere, following the flight of the colorful birds that flitted from tree to tree and seeming to greet the trees themselves. Shafts of sunlight drifted down like—well, like magic—as the wood closed in around us.

When we came to a small rill that chuckled to itself as it ran over a bed of stones, she paused. "Here."

I agreed. The place was private, out of sight from the coach and the road. Like one in a dream, Constanze stood and turned in a circle once more, this time with her eyes closed and her arms held out. She seemed to be absorbing the deep silence that was made up of sounds—the gurgling of the stream, the rustle of branches as the breeze moved through them, and the songs of the birds.

Not wishing to speak and ruin her enjoyment, I set the basket down and let her be. How long passed I do not know. But I saw Constanze change before my eyes. The last of the tension flowed out of her. Her chin came up, and she began to smile…a smile such as I had never before seen on her face.

It looked—and felt—precisely like magic. Not Timor's sort, perhaps. Not magic that coerced or forced, or drove hundreds to their deaths, but something far more subtle that might just be part of the fabric which made up the world.

A city Rat from the day of my birth, it shouldn't have affected me. Yet I felt it begin to seep into me through the fur I now lacked. Did I yet lack it? With the balm of the breeze rushing over me, I swear if I closed my eyes I could still sense the Rat I had been.

"Peace," Constanze spoke suddenly, whispering the word so it sounded like it came from the breeze. "There is peace here, Marquell."

"Yes."

"I cannot tell you how I have needed this." The tears had dried on her cheeks. She held out her fingers as if she drew the feel of the wood into her, and she breathed deeply, seeking the air.

Happiness rose inside me such as I'd never known. Happiness because I had made her happy. I understood, then, a little of why Timor did what he did—whatever he could, to make Elissabet happy.

He loved her.

Did I love Constanze?

At that moment, with the breeze caressing my nonexistent fur and the song of the wood in my ears, it seemed impossible not to love her. Since the days back with my littermates, I'd not been so close to anyone. Her happiness mattered to me; it had become my own.

I sat with my eyes half closed and my legs—Man's legs—stretched out before me while she took her fill of the place. How long it was, I do not know. At last she came and knelt beside me.

She looked changed. Her eyes held a measure of serenity, and reflected the colors all around us, sparks of green for the leaves, gold and russet from the ones that had begun to change. Her eyes, so I saw, were like the water in the rill, alive and ever-changing.

"Thank you, Marquell." She captured my paw between her hands and pressed it to her heart. "Can you feel my happiness?"

I could. I nodded.

"I needed this," she repeated. "It is a balm to my spirit."

"Let us walk," I bade her. "We have but this afternoon."

We strolled through the woodland, taking our time. I let Constanze choose the way, warning only, "We cannot allow ourselves to get lost."

"I could never get lost here."

After, we ate the supper she'd packed for us—savory meat turnovers and sweetmeats filched from the kitchen. The light began to fade.

"Constanze, we need to go back."

She sighed. "I know. Allow me but a few moments more. I need to soak this into me for—for later."

She closed her eyes and drank deep of the air. Everyone, I suppose, belongs somewhere. That place may be just a memory in the back of one's mind, but still it exerts a powerful influence.

Constanze had learned to love the forest while young. It had never since released her.

Softly I said, "I wish I could give you this for always."

She opened her eyes and gave me a smile so beautiful it speared me through. "You have given it to me now." She rose and reached for my hand. "Come, let us go home."

"Is it home?"

"A fair question. Elissabet with her weeping and her constant demands, the insistence that everything—*everything* revolves around her happiness and unhappiness. It may not be home to me as this place is. But with you there, I can endure it."

I thought about those words as we rode back to the

house in Regis Towne, sitting close together. Constanze laid her head on my shoulder, cuddling close.

I did not know how to tell her I might be leaving once my agreement with Timor—that which had bought her this day—elapsed.

I did not know if I should.

Chapter Sixteen

"She will drive me mad, Marquell. I swear by all that is holy, she will."

A mere day and a half had passed since my afternoon in the country with Constanze. The serenity gleaned there had not lasted long.

I had watched Constanze's peace erode, and a terrible thing it was to behold. Imagine a smooth, beautiful surface being eaten away by droplets of acid flung upon it. That was Constanze, and it hurt me almost as much as it hurt her.

I must say I did not quite understand why she let Elissabet bother her so. Granted, I did not like Timor or Elissabet very well despite their flashes of supposed friendliness toward us. Timor was a heartless murderer and Elissabet so hopelessly selfish it nearly defied comprehension.

But Constanze knew what they were, in particular knew what Elissabet was. They'd been together from childhood.

I wished she could grow a thicker skin and shrug off some of the behaviors and demands as I tried to do. She could not.

At the moment, Elissabet was obsessed with her wedding gown. This morning she and Constanze had made the rounds of dressmakers in the town, searching for one who could give Elissabet the fantastical gown she required, and produce it in the time allowed.

"They offered her gowns," Constanze told me in disgust after they returned home. "But not what she wants. She wants miles of tulle and lace spilling into a train, and with pearls covering every inch. Oh, if I hear about that train one more time! And do you know how long it takes to sew on that many pearls?"

I did not. But I was well aware the date of the wedding was only three weeks away. Replies to the invitations had already begun coming in—many acceptances.

I suspected the majority of those invited—the higher echelon of Regis society—were merely coming out of curiosity. I'd overheard enough at the market to know folks still spoke in derisive tones of my master and mistress and even laughed behind their backs when they thought I could not hear. Rats have very keen hearing, indeed.

"Sit down," I bade Constanze now and drew a chair out from the table. "You have been on your feet all day. Let me bring you a cup of tea."

She collapsed into the chair with a sigh, and I prepared the tea. As I set it in front of her, I asked, "Can Timor afford a dress covered in pearls?"

I knew Timor would spend any amount to make Elissabet happy. I will admit that, try as I might, I couldn't keep that from bothering me. The riches Timor had acquired by murdering my family shouldn't be frittered away on a garment worn by a single woman on a single day. But, I began to learn, such was Timor's nature. I imagine he thought there were countless towns like Regis, and countless other Rats to be killed. Easy come, easy go.

Mistress Elissabet's wedding dress, though, would be purchased in blood.

Constanze toyed with her cup but did not drink. Her eyes fastened on my face when I sat down opposite her.

"This morning when we were doing the rounds of the shops, she asked me whether I could make her wedding cake. Me! I told her I'm no fancy baker and could not possibly turn out something that would please her, large enough for a hundred guests. I do not doubt we will be touring the bakeries next, searching out one willing to offer her a good price."

"It will be all right. She cannot possibly expect you to perform duties so far beyond your capabilities."

"That is how it is. From the very beginning, she has expected me to follow her and serve her every unreasonable demand. To live my life for her sake." Constanze waved her hands wildly. "When I try to tell her no, that some task is beyond me, she refuses to hear it. She refuses to hear *me*."

"Yes." They both did it, acted as if only their own desires mattered. I understood Constanze's resentment, but I did not want to see it burn her up.

I captured her wildly flailing hand in mine. "It will pass. All things do." Even my extended commitment to Timor. What would happen after he finally turned me back into a Rat, when I left Constanze for good? Upon whom would she rely then?

The very idea made me shudder. I could barely endure the thought of abandoning her. I'd come to care for her deeply. Yet I was not the Man she thought. If she came to find out what I was in truth, she would scarcely sit so, with her hand resting in mine.

"Things pass, yes, Marquell, but other things come and take their place. Often times much worse things." She lifted her clear eyes to my face. "Have you ever thought about leaving their service? Just running away? I do, constantly."

I thought about leaving their service, yes, but not in the way she meant.

"Run away?" I repeated softly. "And go where?"

"That is the question, isn't it? All these years in service to her, and I own nothing—have nothing of my own. Aside from the coins I've squirreled away, I have earned only my bread and a load of misery."

True. When I left, I could disappear back into my old life. It did still call to me. I dreamed of returning to the space beneath our old house where I'd been born and raised. It would be lonely, yes, with everyone else gone, and doubly so after being accustomed to Constanze's company. But as I say, it did call to me, and I could imagine no other ultimate end.

I would die a Rat, as I'd been born.

I caressed Constanze's fingers gently. "This wedding will come and go. Life will return to its usual quiet. That is not so bad, is it?"

"I do not want to live as her servant any longer. What I want—"

The door from the dining room opened, and Timor came in. Constanze's hand and mine sprang apart as if we'd been scalded, but Timor had very quick eyes, and I knew he had seen.

He gave me a strange look indeed before he said, "Marquell, a word with you, if you please."

I got to my feet. "Yes, Master."

"I have here a list of the foods for the wedding, that

Elissabet has drawn up. I want you to look through it and decide what can be ordered ahead and what must wait for the day. Then go around the shops and do your—er—magic."

His eyes sparkled at me as if he found this humorous.

"Do you forget, Master, I cannot read?"

"Constanze can help you with that part of it. Oh, and Constanze—can you sew? Never mind, I know you can. I have seen you at work mending Elissabet's clothes."

"Master Timor—" Constanze arose also and turned to face him. "I do mending here and there. I am no seamstress. If you are going to ask me to make her wedding dress—"

"Would it be so difficult for you?"

"Yes."

"She will work with you on the design. And of course we will spare no expense with the fabrics. But I think you had better get to work on it at once, if it's to be done in time."

Constanze tipped up her chin. She looked so small, so frail standing there facing him. "I cannot."

"Oh, come. She is your dearest friend. Can you not do this one thing for her?"

"This *one* thing?"

"Yes. She is upstairs weeping because no one can supply the gown of her dreams."

"Her dreams?"

Timor now gave her a strange look. "Yes. And that is what concerns us, is it not? Making Elissabet's dreams come true."

I thought Constanze would shatter. So rigid had she

116

become, so tightly were her fists clenched, I believed she might break apart into pieces that could never be reassembled.

Then I would be completely alone.

"It is too much," I said hoarsely.

"Eh?" Timor switched his gaze to me.

"You ask too much of Constanze, both you and Mistress Elissabet do."

"Oh?" His gaze sharpened. "And what do you know of it?"

"Only what I see. What I feel. It is unreasonable to expect one person to ready the house, prepare a hundred meals, bake the cake, *and* sew the gown." Surely he must see that.

"One person?" His eyes narrowed at me. "She has your assistance, doesn't she? Doesn't she?"

In that instant I saw it all—the power he wielded. He knew what Constanze meant to me. He knew he could tell her I was a Rat—or worse, change me back into one before her eyes. Already I heard her screams in my head and beheld her disgust.

"No," I whispered.

"No? She does not have your help?" He spread his hands, those dangerous hands. "And here was I, thinking you were friends. Then again, I thought the two of you were *our* friends and cared what happened to us."

Constanze trembled so hard I feared she might fall down where she stood.

"Such selfishness," Timor said and wagged his head in wholly feigned reproach.

At that instant, blindingly, I beheld what made Constanze so angry, what ate at her like a sickness, and my determination to not let it bother me flew. He dared speak of selfishness, he who would burn Constanze up—burn the both of us up like candles, at his pleasure.

"Marquell." He looked hard at me. "You know what is at stake."

I did. Elissabet's happiness, around which his revolved. Without Elissabet, he could not be content. And he'd convinced himself that if displeased, she would not stay with him.

Whether or not that was true, I could not say. I'd come to learn that, in his world, reputation was everything. Had I not been trading on his reputation as a wizard all this while, in the market?

The female Men of Regis Towne snickered at Elissabet and laughed behind their hands because she lived with Timor without benefit of marriage. A female Man of quality did not do such a thing. Could she, thus, afford to leave him?

No matter. He believed she would. And belief was everything.

No fool, Timor. He was a master at gauging his audience, and he measured our response now.

His voice softened and took on a quality of wheedling, rather than demand. "Come, you two. This wedding will not be easy for Elissabet. She will have none of her family here. You especially, Constanze, know this. You *are* her family."

"I am not," Constanze said, though her defiance had begun to crumble into hopelessness.

"You most certainly are—her dearest sister. I should think it an honor to make her wedding gown for her."

A blind Man could see Constanze did not consider

it an honor.

"Say you will do whatever you can for her."

Constanze said nothing at all.

After a doubtful look at her, I told Timor, "We will need help to accomplish all this. You must hire someone."

"To be sure, on the day."

"No, before then. You must hire extra staff immediately."

"Very well, just to please you. Am I not a good master?"

He strolled out, having got what he wanted. I had to hold Constanze in my arms as she wept and lamented.

"It is impossible. I cannot do it. The cake! The gown!"

"We will do our best. If it does not get done in time, she will have half a cake on the day and a half-sewn gown."

She nodded, but I had to hold her a long time before she calmed.

If only others could see inside us as I could see inside Constanze, past the mask of appearance, the shield of attitude. Would it make those with whom we share our lives kinder, or still more cruel?

I will never know.

Chapter Seventeen

After that, Constanze sewed. In every spare moment, when not busy at some other task, she sat at the table and stitched like a madwoman.

No more sitting holding hands for us. Not that we could have anyway, for Berta came into the household the very next day, Timor making a big fanfare about keeping his promise.

I do not know where Timor found her for hire, but he did produce her. A young woman surely not above sixteen Man years or so, she appeared the opposite of Constanze in every way—broad and strapping where Constanze was delicate, slow moving in both thought and action where Constanze was quick. She went to work in the kitchen, so we could scarcely have held hands.

From the very first, she frustrated Constanze. Berta took her time accomplishing any tasks she might be given and rarely did them well. She could cook, and did take over that duty. She could haul great pots of water and scrub the floor but never thought to undertake a job she hadn't been given.

Elissabet's mood, however, improved. She and Constanze had gone over designs for her wedding gown, the drawings spread out upon the dining room table. The fabric had been ordered and delivered. Pieces had been cut out. Elissabet seemed to feel the rift between her and Constanze had been mended.

I knew it had not. I could feel Constanze's resentment—it went into every stitch of that gown. A terrible legacy for a wedding dress, as I supposed.

Great lists had been drawn up and pinned to the wall in the kitchen—not just the first listing of the foodstuffs we should need on the day but a full menu, a seating chart that filled in as the acceptances came back, and a long, carefully written accounting of all the chores needing to be done.

I of course could not read these. But I knew much of what they said, for Constanze would peruse them like a person in a trance and repeat them over to herself.

Otherwise she did not talk to me as she once had or complain about the unfairness of it all. That worried me. I had come to know Constanze, had seen her furious, annoyed, irritated, and most of all resentful.

Her emotions now seemed to reach beyond all these and rendered her mostly silent, even on the rare occasions we were alone.

One morning a week or so before the wedding, I poked my head into the kitchen and found Constanze there by herself. In the old days she might have tossed me a smile. She would most definitely have hurried to give me breakfast and sat with me while I ate it. Now I expected no such thing, and indeed, she went right on stitching when I asked, "Where is Berta?"

"Sweeping the walk and the steps out front. It may take her an age, but at least she will get every scrap of dust."

"Something you will not need to do." I entered the room. "How goes the gown?"

"I am nearly finished with the seams. Elissabet will

need to try it on before I stitch up the last of them. Then there's the finishing."

"Finishing?"

"All the lace and pearls."

It would never be done in time. I did not say so. She looked very tired, her eyes red and her cheeks pale. I wished I could take her out for the day. Impossible.

"It will all be over soon, Constanze."

"Yes, for better or worse. There is toast and a bowl of porridge that I saved for you on the back of the stove."

I sat on a stool well away from the table and ate, not wishing to soil the yards and yards of fabric heaped upon the scrubbed table. I had been informed it was not white but ivory satin, of first quality.

Timor had by now been paid the balance of his fee, that earned by murdering my kind. I should be free. Instead I sat and ate his fare and worked in his service. All for the sake of a female Man—that should have been my most devoted enemy. Constanze.

She might not speak to me often these days, but she appreciated me. I could feel that in spite of her misery—her gratitude for my presence flowed from her just the way her resentment did and was in her every glance at me.

What if she found out the truth about me—that I was a Rat? Would that change everything? I'd never been as close to anyone as I was to Constanze. Not my cousins or siblings in my youth. Certainly not my Father, who'd had very little to do with me. Not even my Mother, after my first weeks of life.

I could not underestimate Constanze's importance to me or underrate how I would miss her when all this came to an end.

She broke the silence to ask, "Why do you look at me that way?"

"What way?"

She bit off the thread and re-threaded the needle. "As if you're looking inside me."

"Am I doing that?"

"Yes."

I liked looking at her. I could not say why. She held none of the attributes of a female Rat. When it came down to it, she held none of the flash and sparkle of a female Man either. But watching the movements of her hands pleased me, as did catching the emotions in her pale eyes.

"I am sorry."

She smiled suddenly, and it changed her, lit her from within. "Do not be."

"I don't wish to discomfit you."

She shook her head. "It helps me, knowing you care. It helps me, knowing you're there. Ha! I made a poem."

I tipped my head, not sure what a poem might be.

"I suppose that is what friends do, eh, Marquell? Be constant to one another through all things."

Through all things? Even a deception? I should tell her the truth about myself. Our friendship, as she said, might well endure it. But now when she was so frazzled and could barely take time to listen to me was not the moment.

"Yes," I said softly instead and finished my porridge, which I enjoyed very much. "Have you things I can do to help you today? I have only to accompany Timor on a small job, brush his good suit, clean his shoes, and bring in a load of coal."

"Only that."

"Nothing to keep me from helping you."

She stopped sewing and gazed at me. "I ask again, Marquell, what would I do without you?"

****

I saw her again late that afternoon when she told me the fitting for the wedding gown had gone well and Elissabet seemed pleased. Elissabet, of course, had spent most the day lounging in her boudoir, and I could only sympathize with Constanze's aggravation.

She was set to begin sewing on the lace and then the pearls.

Elissabet, so she said, was eager for it to be finished as soon as possible.

I went off to move the last of the coal, worried in my heart and mind. I feared Constanze would at the very least ruin her health over this and at the very worst sustain lasting damage in her heart and mind.

It was late the next afternoon I overheard a conversation not meant for my ears. Berta did not chatter often. She performed the tasks given with considerable prodding, and ventured little. Perhaps that is what caught my ear when, passing by the kitchen door, I heard her speaking within. Or maybe it was hearing my own name.

"That Marquell is a funny sort of creature, is he not?"

I froze in mid-step and peered into the room.

Constanze sat at the table. She'd begun sewing on the lace, and yards of it spilled across her lap.

Berta stood at the stove, chopping carrots into a pot, speaking over her shoulder to Constanze, who looked up sharply.

"Whatever do you mean, Berta?"

"Well he don't look right, do he?"

Constanze's needle faltered. "Is there a right or wrong in how we look? People are all different. Take you and me, for example. Could we be more different?"

"What I mean is, that Marquell—well, he don't look quite human."

Constanze's needle faltered again, and her hands began to tremble. "Don't say such things."

Berta ignored the command. "He looks like some sort of animal. A rat, maybe."

Perhaps it took an outsider arriving with fresh sight to see things clearly. True, I'd been to the market and around with Timor when he did his jobs. Folk did always give me odd looks. But for Berta to say such a thing—

She went on. "That funny, narrow face of his, and that pointy nose. Even his black eyes. Have you seen how they glitter? Right ugly he is."

I dropped the coal scuttle from my hand. It didn't make a great noise—Berta missed it. But Constanze turned her head, and our eyes met through the doorway.

Could she see what I was at that moment? A Rat grown to monstrous size, up on his back feet and wearing a footman's garb. Could she see the truth of me at last?

She turned her face back to Berta, pretending I was not there. "It is not kind," she told the maid, "to belittle the appearance of others. To make fun of them."

"I am not making fun," Berta denied. "I only say what is true. Marquell has a ratty face."

"He is the steward of this house and deserves your

respect."

"Yes, Constanze."

"Anyway, you should never fault people for things they cannot help or change. Those are things you should strive to overlook."

And was that how Constanze felt toward me? Did she overlook my strange appearance for the sake of our friendship? For kindness? I flattened myself against the wall, but I did not move away, desiring to hear what was said.

I had hoped she might take pleasure in looking at me as I took in looking at her. A futile hope, it seemed. Constanze went on, "Would you like it, Berta, if I faulted you for your appearance?"

"Mine, Constanze?"

"Yes, if I said your hair was dull and mousy, that you plodded around the place like an ox, or that your figure resembled a bag of pudding tied in the middle?"

"No, Constanze!"

I stifled a laugh, pressed there against the wall. Constanze's defense of me was as fierce as all her other emotions. I relaxed a bit and felt better.

Should it be an insult, Berta saying I looked like a Rat? I *was* a Rat. And Rats—well, we deal always in reality.

Chapter Eighteen

"I overheard you defending me," I told Constanze later that evening when we met in the yard. Dusk was just falling, and she'd come out to shake the rugs. She looked very tiny, silhouetted by the light from the kitchen, and tired.

I was bringing in Timor's coats, which had aired on the line. "Thank you."

"No need for thanks." She sniffed. "Berta does not often say much. When she does, she betrays her ignorance."

She cocked an eye at me and folded the rug over her arm. "Anyway, what one person may find unattractive, another might like very much indeed. Marquell, you know what I think of you. At least I hope you do."

I looked down at my dusty feet. "I know you have offered me your friendship, which I appreciate very much."

"It is more than friendship, what I feel."

I looked up at her. For several moments we gazed at one another while the air grew ever darker around us.

"Marquell," she whispered then, "you must know I—I have come to have strong feelings for you. Indeed, I have come to love you."

The darkness around me spun. Rats understand the concept of love—never let it be thought we do not. My

Mother had squeaked lovingly to me when I was still in the nest, and other family members, so I believed, showed their affection both by sharing and by their concern. No one had ever told me they loved me.

I did not know how to respond. I stepped up onto the stoop where she stood and took her in my arms, rug and all.

We stood there while her emotions beat at me as they always did—not anger or resentment this time but just as intense. Her caring unwound from her and wrapped around me. She pressed close and held me fiercely tight.

"I don't care how you look," she whispered after several moments passed. "I care who you are. Anyway, I quite like the way you look."

"Do you?"

She tipped up her head so she could gaze at me. Her eyes looked pale as starlight, all the weariness gone. "Would you like me to show you?"

Without waiting for an answer she kissed me. Such a strange sensation. Rats do not kiss. We nuzzle and sometimes nip or groom one another.

I now inhabited the body of a Man, however, like it or not. And that body responded of its own accord to the feel of her mouth on mine.

A gentle sort of kiss it was. Constanze, unlike Berta or myself, used a lot of words—though she had lately been loud in her silence. This kiss said far more than any words could.

It said, *I want to be near you. You bring me happiness. Whatever else happens in my world, I value you and want you here.*

"I'm glad you are here," she said the last of it aloud

once the kiss ended. "And I hope you know...I hope you know I quite like the foreign look of you."

I nodded, all my ability to vocalize stolen by the sweetness of her gesture.

Tucking her head in against my neck, she clutched me still more tightly. "Marquell, say you will not forsake me."

Would it be forsaking her if after the wedding I held Master Timor to his promise and turned back into what I truly was?

What could I tell her? She needed reassurance at that moment, and I was her friend.

"I will not forsake you. Not so long as you want me with you."

****

Excitement built as the day of the wedding approached. All the acceptances had been returned; there were to be more than ninety guests. Tables were set up in the dining room and the back parlor, and all the food stuffs were ordered. Elissabet flitted around the house from one room to another, talking about the flowers and where they would be situated.

The ceremony would take place in the garden at the side of the house—not the rather squalid enclosed yard where we hung our laundry and sometimes met to converse.

I was set the task of weeding the beds with the help of a young lad named Karl, who would also serve on the day. It was a task I did not mind, as I discovered somewhat to my surprise. The formal garden beds were peaceful, and I enjoyed putting my paws in the dirt.

The peace was shattered one afternoon only two days before the wedding when a piercing scream came from the house.

Karl and I both heard it and popped up from separate flower beds several rows apart.

"My God, Master Steward, what was that?"

I did not bother to answer. A second shriek followed the first, and another, and another.

I scrambled up and went over the wall into the back yard. I did it as a Rat might, using my fingers and toes to get to the top before leaping in.

The kitchen door stood open. The screaming came from within.

I should have known that, given all the pressures upon us, everything would come to a head. I might have guessed one single event would prompt the eruption. But what an event!

And what a scene met my eyes when I entered the kitchen!

Constanze had been sitting at the table when I'd left the room, sewing on the last of the tiny pearls for the wedding dress. She'd been pushing hard to finish among myriad other tasks, staying up late and starting early, stealing every moment she could.

Now the dress lay heaped across the table, luminescent with pearls and frothing with lace, a sea of ivory except—

Except for a large brown stain spread across a great swath of it.

Constanze and Berta stood facing each other across the table, Berta still with the teapot in her hands and a vacant look on her rather bovine face.

Timor and Elissabet, who had come running as had I, posed in the doorway of the dining room looking aghast. Constanze—

Constanze appeared as I had never seen her, a person transformed, face stretched in a rictus as she continued to shriek, the words pouring from her.

"You cow! You stupid, clumsy cow! What have you done? Oh, I shall kill you for this. I shall!"

Constanze leaped over the broad table, over the garment spread upon it, and straight for Berta's throat. Her small hands turned into claws, her eyes spat fire, and at that moment I believed Berta, nearly twice her size, would perish beneath her assault.

"Ruined!" She half-screamed, half-sobbed as she leaped. "You have ruined it!"

Timor and I both moved at once. Even as Berta fell backward, her expression at last altering to one of horror, I laid hands upon Constanze, who had turned into a shrieking, flailing menace. She rained blows upon the bigger girl, still reaching for her throat, and the pain of her cries was unfettered.

I laid hold of the back of her dress, reaching for her shoulders, my one aim to protect her from her own anger and grief. Timor tried to insert his body between the two of them. But Constanze was strong. She'd become fury incarnate. And try as I might, I could not keep her seeking hands from their goal.

We all went down onto the flagstone floor of the kitchen, Berta flat on her back with Constanze atop her, still shrieking like a madwoman, I still trying to contain her, and Timor trapped by the two of them.

Unable to get a fair purchase on Berta's neck, Constanze used her fingers like talons to gouge the maid's face. Blood stood out like paint on Berta's doughy skin. I'd rarely seen such fear in anyone's eyes.

"Stop it!" Timor snapped, having extracted himself

somehow and sitting up. He slapped Constanze across the face, trying I suppose to shock her out of her hysteria. An ugly gesture, it made me feel even more protective, and a snarl ripped from my throat.

He looked at me. I felt a little frisson of magic wash over us. Constanze went suddenly limp, and I was able to get my arms around her and draw her away.

She was not unconscious. I could still feel the anger coursing through her, the wild grief that filled her to the brim. Constanze rarely lost control of her emotions. They'd gone fully off their lead this time.

Yet she allowed me to hold her, to wrap my arms tight around her from behind, though she never took her gaze from Berta, who lay in a heap.

Constanze breathed hard and so did I, the shock and alarm still pounding through me. Timor half knelt, and Elissabet stood frozen in the doorway, hand to her lips.

"Hush. Hush," I told Constanze over and over again.

She had blood on her hands, as I saw when I sought to capture them in mine. And blood still oozed down Berta's face. Berta's eyes stared like two black stones. The teapot had landed on the floor during the attack and shattered. A pool of hot tea spread at Timor's knee.

Surveying all this, Elissabet spoke, and her words displayed in full her utter selfishness. "My wedding dress!"

Yes, I suppose any bride might do the same under the circumstances. And I cannot here reproduce her tone, which expressed no concern for any other party involved.

Even Timor, I think, picked up on the staggering self-centeredness of it, for he glanced at me when he asked Berta, "Are you hurt?"

Before she could answer, Constanze began shrieking again. She screamed out her misery, which as I knew had started accumulating long before the wedding dress ever came to be, and decried Berta's clumsiness over again. She wept out her desperation and pain, which had turned itself into bitterness and hate.

All aimed at the hapless Berta.

It did seem unreasonable, such an attack. Berta had not meant to slop tea on the gown or spoil it. And again it did not seem unreasonable, given the cost to Constanze of making that dress.

"Hush," I continued to beg Constanze, my cheek pressed against hers.

But she would not quiet, and Timor snapped at me, "Get her out of here. Take her up to her room."

I knew where Constanze's room lay, at the back of the attic, though I'd never been there. She tried to fight me as I drew her away, her strength astounding. In the end I had to lift her up and carry her in my arms.

As we left the kitchen, pushing past Elissabet, I heard Elissabet say, "Oh, Timor, my gown! I think I am going to faint."

Constanze started to quiet as I carried her through the house, up the stairs, and along the corridors. She remained rigid in my arms, though, and I could no longer feel her breathing. It frightened me.

"Constanze? Constanze, speak to me."

She made a terrible sound in her throat, one of grief. I did not think she grieved solely for the dress.

I pushed open the door of her chamber with my foot, carried her in, and set her on the bed. A small, barren place this, no fit reward for Constanze's hours upon hours of labor. It sported only a single straight-backed chair and a washstand, in addition to the bed, which might be better called a cot, and a single narrow window letting in the light.

I knelt before Constanze and held her hands. "Look at me, Constanze. Look at me. Are you hurt?"

"Yes!" she wailed. "Yes, I am hurt. I am destroyed! Can't you see that, Marquell?"

I could. She did not speak of physical hurts but harm that struck far more deeply.

"They have used me up. Used me up! I can take no more."

A breaking point had in fact come. And she had broken.

Eyes wild, she seized hold of my hand and then my arm. "Take me away from here, Marquell. Please, please, take me away. I can no longer stay."

"Take you? Where?"

"Back to the forest. Take me back to the wood. I can breathe there. If I remain here I will perish."

"I would that I could. I have no means—"

"We can stay in the hovel where we spent our afternoon. We can live among the trees, for all that. I do not need much. I need only peace."

"Constanze, Timor will not allow it."

"Curse Timor!" she howled.

Yes, curse him from his head to his toes. But we had not that power.

"Constanze, listen to me. If we run from here, he will come after us. He will seek us by magic and other means."

"I do not belong to him."

But in a way, we did—not through ownership, perhaps, but by necessity.

"I want to be free," she told me through gritted teeth. Her eyes no longer looked like her own. Her skin had gone patchy, hectic red against the pasty white.

Fixing her wild gaze on mine she said, "I want to kill them all. That thick cow, Berta. Timor, with his smug smiles, and—and Elissabet most of all." She held up her hands and cried, like a child, "See what she has done to me!"

I will freely confess, I did not know what to do, how to comfort her or deal with such flagrant emotions. I did know she could let no one else hear her talk so, nobody but me.

"Hush, Constanze, hush. You mustn't say such things." If she threatened Elissabet and Timor aloud, Timor might decide to deal with her. I knew the cold that lodged at his heart and of what he was capable. He might do anything to her.

And then…then I would be utterly alone.

Perhaps it truly is selfishness that motivates us all. Elissabet with her self-centered lack of ability to sense the emotions of others. Timor with his need to possess Elissabet's beauty at any cost. Me needing Constanze to answer a terrifying loneliness.

What did Constanze need? Her freedom, so she said. I could not give her that. All I could offer her was me. And I possessed not the arrogance to suppose that alone could save her.

"Listen. Listen to me. You cannot say such things—that you wish to harm them." I jerked my head at the door. "Not within their hearing. Say what you like to me—but you must be careful."

"I have been careful." Her eyes glowed with rage. "I have bitten my tongue until it is ragged. I have endured the unbearable. Where has it got me?"

"If Timor thinks you might harm Elissabet, things will become worse."

She gave a crazed laugh. "Worse? How can they?"

"He will turn you over to the authorities. Lock you away. Be quiet." My ears—so very sharp—heard a step in the hallway outside the chamber. Without warning, the door swung open.

Timor stood there. He looked shocked and disheveled, a cold light in his pied eyes. To be utterly truthful, he looked dangerous.

His gaze flew to Constanze, completely overlooking me, though it is to me he spoke. "I have summoned the constables."

"What?" I sprang to my feet. I think I had the vague notion of protecting Constanze by putting myself between her and Timor. Foolish, of course.

I have learned there are moments in life, terrible moments, when one's worst fears come true. I'd suffered one such when I saw the Rats of Regis jumping into the harbor. Another now.

"Please, Master Timor, no—"

"She has gone mad." He waved a hand, and I flinched, all too aware of what his magic could do.

For an instant he fastened that cold, terrifying gaze upon me. "She must be locked away."

Chapter Nineteen

Timor and I faced each other outside the closed door of Constanze's chamber. We'd stepped out of the room when she once more began raving about Berta and the ruined wedding dress.

She did herself no favors.

"Master Timor, please," I said, ignoring the wild wailing from within. "Constanze is deeply upset."

"She is deeply disturbed."

"She worked so hard at making that dress. She works hard to make everything in this house happen. For Berta to ruin it at the last moment—"

"It is no excuse for her to fly at the maid."

It was, only I didn't know how to make him see it. Things tended to pile up on a person. Slight upon slight, casual insult upon casual insult, sacrifice upon sacrifice. A breaking point was reached. A person's true nature, tamped down so long, spewed out.

"What if she flies at Elissabet that way? Scratches her beautiful face? Gouges her eyes?"

"Is Berta all right?"

"She will heal. She may be marked, however. I have summoned the physician. When he arrives, he will see Constanze also."

"Please no, Master Timor," I beseeched again. "They may take her away from here, lock her away—"

"As they should, if she might harm Elissabet." Still

no concern for Constanze. There never had been. Not after all the years of service and supposed friendship.

"Allow her to compose herself, to settle down. She lost her temper, that is all."

"And am I to allow her to remain near Elissabet? Alone with her in her bedchamber? Caring for her? Constanze has gone mad. Yes, we all lose our tempers, Marquell. Even I. And when I do, dire things tend to happen. If she were to harm Elissabet, Constanze would consider herself fortunate to be locked away from me."

He gave me a hard look. "You know of what I am capable."

I did. A spear of cold passed through me, followed by heat. He could use his magic upon Constanze to turn her into anything. A Roach. A Pig. A Cat.

"Master Timor, being shut away somewhere would kill her." I thought of Constanze's expression when she looked at the stars out in the yard. Of her happiness among the trees of the wood.

At that moment I tasted Constanze's bitterness in full, that which always accompanied her like a scent. I experienced her anger and felt her wounds.

Timor lowered his voice. "There is an asylum in the town. I am sure the physician will determine whether that is the best place for Constanze."

"Asylum?" I questioned.

"You do not know what that is? A secure place where they lock away mad men and women."

No doubt the physician would determine Constanze belonged there, once Timor spoke with him, gave him that hard look, and made him realize where his best interest lay.

I tried to imagine it. Shut into some narrow

chamber or cell. Away from the bright air, away from the trees and sky. How long would it take Constanze to perish?

My heart twisted in my chest. I could not allow it.

Yet I understood the futility of trying to argue it further with Timor. He knew nothing of mercy, and his mind was made up.

"Keep her quiet till they arrive, if you can," he told me, and stalked off.

I stood where I was for several moments, wondering what I should do. What I could do. With nothing decided, I went back into the room.

Constanze paced the tiny chamber. She did look like a madwoman at this point, all her hair yanked out from its customary neat bun—by her own hands, as I saw when she tugged at it. That hectic flush still rode her face, and tension stiffened every limb. Her eyes— but I have no words to describe the expression there.

"Constanze," I whispered.

She didn't hear me. Or, more likely, she disregarded me. She paced like an animal in a trap. I had a terrible, clear vision of her doing just this for days uncounted if they locked her away.

"Constanze, listen to me. Perhaps the dress can be cleaned."

Her step faltered. She turned her head and looked at me. "This is not about the dress."

I knew that. I knew it wasn't. It was about all the injustices of the past piled one atop the other. It was about insufferable selfishness and a weight too heavy to bear.

She looked directly at me. "I hate them. I want to kill them all."

"Do not say that, Constanze. Do not let them catch a hint of such talk, or they will lock you up. Already Timor speaks of an asylum—"

"I heard. I have very good hearing."

"Then, on your life, get hold of yourself. You must appear calm when the physician comes, so he will let you stay here. With me."

She began pacing once more, eyes wild.

"Please, Constanze. I will go downstairs and talk with Elissabet. Surely, despite everything, she will take your part."

Constanze laughed. I'd heard her do so in the past at some quip I made. Never like this.

"You expect mercy? From Elissabet?"

"She will not want to lose you, especially now." Elissabet needed her, on the doorstep of the wedding. Elissabet relied upon her. Surely I could talk her round.

"Sit down, Constanze, please. Let me speak with her. The two of you are so close—"

Constanze bared her teeth at me. No smile, this.

I went out, shutting the door firmly behind me. I took the back stairs down and went through the kitchen. The wedding dress still lay on the table, marred by the ecru stain, and the teapot was in pieces on the floor. Of Berta, there was no sign.

My ears directed me to the parlor, where I found both Elissabet and Timor. Elissabet lay prostrate on the sofa, one arm bent across her forehead, bemoaning her predicament.

"My dress! What am I to do, Timor? There is no time to procure another one."

"Wear something else, my love. You will be beautiful beyond compare, no matter what you wear."

"I cannot get married without a wedding dress." Her wail increased in pitch and volume. "All those people coming! She has destroyed everything."

"Mistress Elissabet," I whispered, "a word, if you please."

They both stared at me.

"Marquell, what are you doing here?" Timor demanded. "You should be guarding that madwoman."

Elissabet chimed in, "What if she comes down here and attacks me?"

"She won't." In truth I wasn't so certain. I could picture Constanze following my footsteps through the kitchen, picking up a butcher's knife along the way, and going on the attack.

Elissabet sat up. Tears streaked her face, and a moody, stubborn look hovered over her features.

Despite her forbidding manner, I eased into the room. "I beg you, Mistress Elissabet, reconsider sending for the physician or treating Constanze hastily. She was under great strain and lost her temper. We all do from time to time."

"She ruined my dress."

I felt my own ire stir. "Forgive me, but she did not. She made your dress, worked countless hours on it till her fingers near bled. It was Berta who—"

"She attacked a member of this household. How can I trust her ever again?"

"You can. You can! Is she not more your friend than your servant? The two of you have been together so long. How will you ever get by without her?"

"I don't know."

"You need her." Why not appeal to her monstrous selfishness? "You will never get through the wedding unless she is here to help."

"Why do you argue her part?" Elissabet asked waspishly.

"I can see this is but an upset brought on by everyone being—being tired and overwrought. I can see it will all be right again if we calm down."

Timor bent a look at me from his oddly colored eyes. I did not like that look. It told me if I argued too hard or upset Elissabet further, there would be consequences for me as well as Constanze.

He was the only one who could turn me back into a Rat, give me back my own life. At that moment I felt terrified of him.

At that moment I felt terrified of both of them.

"Go back upstairs," Timor told me.

"But—"

"Go upstairs and guard that creature."

Creature? That creature had been Elissabet's comfort countless times, had washed her, dressed her, performed tasks to satisfy her whims, and countless times had sacrificed her own comfort and welfare.

I looked at Elissabet. "Please, Mistress," I whispered.

"I want her out of this house. She is dangerous," Elissabet howled. "How can I have her near me if she's capable of flying off the handle that way? She might attack me." She turned to Timor and held out her hands. "Oh, Timor—protect me!"

"Go," Timor snapped at me.

The last glimpse I had of them was Timor holding Elissabet in his arms while she sobbed and fretted—the very picture of a spoiled child.

Chapter Twenty

I charged up the stairs and into Constanze's chamber, where still she paced and muttered to herself.

"Pack your things. We are leaving."

She turned her gaze on me and blinked. "What?"

"You cannot stay here. Elissabet is—" I waved a hand at the door behind me. "Elissabet is beyond reason. Gather up whatever you need."

When she continued to stare, I took her by the shoulders and cried, "Constanze, they are coming for you."

Those words got through to her. She jerked into motion and began moving around the room, gathering items of clothing, which she rolled into a bundle.

I gave her little time to think. With my keen hearing fixed on the rest of the house, I said, "Hurry. You will have to go out the window. Here, I'll help you."

The ancient sash on the window stuck. I employed brute force, and it creaked open with a terrible groan. I looked out. Straight down from here was the walled garden.

The house being constructed of plaster and beam, there were footholds. Narrow as the window might be, Constanze was a tiny little thing and, I thought, would fit through.

I called her to me and looked into her eyes. "You

are not afraid of the climb?"

She barely glanced at the drop. "No."

"When you get down, run. Get out of sight as quickly as possible. Do you understand? You can let no one see you. Hide behind those trees at the back before you go over the wall." I caught her between my hands and gazed into her eyes, bent on impressing the danger upon her. "Do you think you can climb over?"

"Yes." She gazed back at me, for the first time making a connection. "What about you?"

"I do not know if I can fit through that window. I'll go down through the house and meet you."

Her fingers curled into the front of my coat. "But if they stop you—you'll be caught."

Caught. A word to inspire dread in every Rat's heart. I'd seen plenty of Rats caught in terrible ways. By the tail in a trap. By the paw, by the head. The trap did not always snap the neck, and it caused unimaginable suffering.

I'd seen Rats trapped in a room with no way out save being stomped to death by the large boot of a Man.

My skin prickled all over my body.

"I'll get out. I'll meet you, so I do promise. Go over the back wall and wait for me at the end of the lane that faces the shops."

"No." She tugged my hands. "Come with me."

"I tell you I won't fit."

I could hear voices from below, footsteps, and Elissabet's excited wail. We both heard. Constanze tossed her bundle out the window and scrambled over the sill, still pulling at me.

"You must come."

I felt her desperation just as I felt the danger

stemming from downstairs. I'm not sure which propelled me. Holding her hand, I leaned across the sill and helped lower her down. Agile, she made nothing of the climb, her fingers and toes scrambling, and reached the ground with only a mild bump. She stood with her face raised, looking up at me.

She had the sense to keep from calling out. She didn't need to—the emotions in her eyes persuaded me.

I turned my body and tried to fit through the window. Narrow it was. I could reach out with one arm or the other but the aperture would not admit even my narrow shoulders.

I blessed Elissabet then, with her whining and no doubt lengthy, belabored explanations. It should give me time.

Forcing myself sideways into the casement, I wiggled between the pane and the clasp, which caught on my coat. Fully stuck, I glanced down at Constanze, who still stood directly below me. "Go! Run!"

She slipped away soundlessly, her eyes full of grief. I tried to free myself by going back into the chamber, but I couldn't manage that either. When Timor came into the room and found me—well, I would suffer his wrath. I could scarcely imagine what he might do to me through sheer rage or magic. Not now, of course—he would wait until the physician and any other officials left before he unleashed his displeasure.

Feet on the stairs in the distance. The sound of voices growing nearer.

Rats are very good with small spaces. We can chew our way through most anything or, in a pinch, compress our bodies enough to squeeze through amazingly narrow apertures. So I did now. No longer a Rat, I nevertheless expelled all the air in my chest and made it narrower. I tore my coat and left skin on the casement, but I made it through.

I don't remember scrambling down the outside of the house. I dashed across the overgrown walled garden, hoping to find it empty of Constanze.

But she'd waited for me back under the scrubby trees at the rear of the space. Her hands came out from nowhere and snagged my coat.

"Go. You should go."

"I will now. Boost me up."

I made a stirrup of my hands while looking back at the house. They must be in the room by now and would see the open window. If they looked out, would they spy us?

Constanze went over the wall, agile as—well, as a Rat. The window of her room remained empty. I launched myself up and over, scrabbling, and Constanze seized hold of me as soon as my feet met the ground.

"What now?" she breathed.

"We hide."

Rats are good at that also. I knew a lot of places to hide. Of course many of them were too small to conceal us now, but I knew how to disappear into unused space and shadow.

I seized her hand. "Run."

There is an art to running at the edge of sight, of employing stillness and stealth. I used it to take us across the town, just two small figures gathering no notice. I made for my old stomping ground, which I felt could afford us some places to hide. We dashed, we paused, always—always holding hands.

Only once were we caught out. While rounding a corner, we met a Man coming the other way, a paunchy fellow with a cane and a bright yellow waistcoat. Without hesitation, I pulled Constanze into my arms and kissed her.

He chuckled as he passed us by.

When the kiss ended, Constanze touched my face. "You are bleeding."

"I stuck in the window casement. Come."

I took her to the rear of the house where I used to live. A humble neighborhood, it could not be called prosperous nor particularly well-kept. A good place for Rats and perhaps runaways.

I had lived in a space beneath the floor and had an acquaintance with the Rats who dwelt in the shed. They'd chewed an opening in the back, which faced a wattle fence. Not big enough to admit us, to be sure, but I was able to enlarge the hole by breaking away some of the boards with my hands.

We crawled in.

The shed smelled strongly of the straw stored there, of mud, and of the Rats who used to live here. All gone now, and sorrow touched my heart. Since the death of all Regis's Rats, I'd not ventured into my old haunts or indeed anywhere I might expect to meet others of my kind. I'd been confined to the world of Men. For that reason, I think the full of my grief did not hit me till now.

However, I had Constanze on my hands and could scarcely think of myself. The shed was dim inside, the only light coming from cracks around the door at the front. Between there and us stood heaps of hay and small stacks of firewood.

A good place to hide, at least for now.

My heart—the heart of a Rat—eased. I spread some straw, and Constanze threw herself down on it, her anger and tension giving way to desperate dejection.

She curled into a ball and sobbed. Not sure what to do with a weeping female Man, I sat and rubbed her back with my hand. Events back at the house had occurred so abruptly, I had time only now to contemplate them.

Questions teemed in my mind. Had I done the right thing, taking Constanze away? She had no one but me to protect her. I couldn't let them lock her away from the air, from the sky. What were we to do now, both of us without a home? This shed would do for the night— maybe for several nights—but as an environment, it was little better for Constanze than a cell.

Would she return to her senses, overcome her anger? What if something inside her had indeed broken, and she remained this raving, mad female whom I could not reach?

And the most terrifying question of all: would Timor come after us? Would his outrage at our disobedience and a desire for revenge cause him to hunt us down without mercy? Might he use his magic to find us and to smite us once he did?

The idea made me shiver. And the very thought of his queerly colored eyes, one green and one brown, and the expression they acquired when he worked a spell, near froze me with fear.

Oh, what had I done? I chased it over and over in my head till I arrived at an answer: I had done the only thing I could.

Constanze eventually stopped weeping. I wondered whether she slept, till she suddenly rolled over in the straw to face me.

"You shouldn't have come away with me, Marquell."

"I could not let you go alone, or leave you there to be seized and—and shut away."

"But you have lost your place. You will suffer right along with me."

I told her truthfully, "I would rather go without, in your company, than have walls around me and meals on the table."

"Oh, Marquell!" She clutched my hand, and her eyes flooded with tears.

"Besides, have we not walls around us? And I should be able to steal us some food once it gets dark." I knew how to jiggle the lock and get in the back door of the house. The pantry lay just inside. Of course I was much bigger than I used to be. But I felt confident I could manage.

"Steal?"

"This is my old world," I told her, "from before Timor took me on as his helper. I got by through stealing most my food." It was close as I'd dared come to telling her the truth. Would she be appalled?

She merely nodded. "You were a waif, were you? Grew up on your own?"

"Mostly."

"I knew there was something about you. Something different. I still say you shouldn't have thrown everything away for me—all your security."

"I am happy to be with you."

"And I with you." She smiled at me there in the dusty gloom. It provided me great relief, for in her eyes I could see the old Constanze returning—she who grumped and suffered and complained yet always had a kind word for me, a sweetmeat saved, a gentle touch. The Constanze one saw on the outside, as well I knew, bore little relation to the spirit within, which had become very dear to me.

"I would not have done well in a cell, locked away in an asylum," she reflected.

"No."

"You have saved me from that fate. I will be forever grateful. But what shall we do?"

"You need worry about nothing now. Just rest."

Rest. Sleep, return to herself—become once again the Constanze who was so dear to me.

So she was, the dearest of anyone. A truth that had become clear only when I feared I might lose her.

Chapter Twenty-One

I waited till after dark to break into the kitchen.
While the Men of the house slept, I jiggled the back
door till the latch gave way—everyone knew that latch
was defective—and I crept inside.

How strange it was, being there again! The place
where I'd been raised smelled the same as ever, but so
much else had changed. The perspective, for one
thing—even though I huddled down as I shuffled along,
I saw the rooms and their contents from far too high up.
Added to that, my night vision had drastically declined,
and my body fit nowhere it used to.

Still, the scents brought a rush of memory, of furry
bodies pressed close together in our nest. Mother used
to steal food for us. Now I would steal for Constanze.

But oh, that house felt empty—lifeless despite the
Men sleeping upstairs.

I took cheese and a heel of bread, not too much. I
didn't want the theft to be noticed, since I would need
to visit again. I left with grief in my heart and worry for
Constanze in my mind.

I was right to worry. As I discovered when I
reached the rear of the shed, she might have quieted,
but all was not right with her.

In the past, I had seen Rats panicked. Some had
been trapped and escaped, some chased by screeching
women with brooms or scalded by hot water. Men do

terrible things to my kind.

Afterward, those Rats remained twitchy. They started at the movement of a leaf, and great emotion ranged in their hearts. Usually they did not live long.

When I reached Constanze now, she lay upon the straw. I might be deceived into supposing she slept. But her eyes stared wide in the gloom, and her hands trembled violently.

I helped her sit up. "Here, I brought some food. Are you hungry?"

"No."

"Did you hurt yourself climbing down from the window?"

She shook her head and clutched at me blindly.

"Try to eat something."

"I cannot."

"Rest, then. We are safe here."

I knew that for a lie, even if she did not. We were anything but safe. I wanted to ask her what she thought Timor would do, her acquaintance with him being much longer than mine. But I dared not.

Eventually she spoke in a raw, ugly whisper. "She will blame me for the dress." She was right, as I knew—Elissabet already did blame Constanze.

"It wasn't your fault."

"That doesn't matter. She will blame me anyway. I sometimes think it is why she kept me with her, to have someone to blame."

I stroked her hair. "You are free of her now."

"Am I? Am I free?"

"Yes." It occurred to me that both of us were now free. But I had given up any chance at returning to my true condition.

Constanze clutched me more tightly. "It feels so nice, you stroking my hair."

"Be at ease, Constanze. Go to sleep."

"I will try. So long as you are here, Marquell, I will be all right. I can do anything."

Perhaps, I concluded, there were in fact more important things than being comfortable in one's own skin.

****

Going to ground in my old haunting place had its advantages and disadvantages, as I discovered over the following days. When I'd lived in Timor's world at Timor's behest, it had been possible to push bad thoughts to the back of my mind in order to get through the days.

Here, I had little to do but think. And the changes were all too evident. I might have returned to my world, but it was empty. The spaces that used to teem with Rats, with cousins and friends, lay hollow and barren. I could not dodge the knowledge that they were not only gone but dead.

Constanze's condition also worried me. She pretended to recover from the madness that had seized her—for my sake, she did. I could still feel the emotions that tore at her, though, like a constant storm raging inside. The resentment she'd always carried had burst out of control and would not fit back into the box she'd created for it.

She couldn't pretend in her sleep and often muttered and moaned. She would awaken me with streams of desperate words, for she slept always in my arms.

She slept always in my arms.

How can I explain what she meant to me? I had not expected it—forced into Timor's household and myself bereft, I had not thought to become attached to, of all creatures, a female Man. But we had suffered together. We had survived together. As I'd become her solace, she had become mine.

I discovered that truth somewhere along the days we spent shut away in the rear of the shed, which still smelled of those I had known. All ghosts now. Constanze still existed, no ghost, and she needed me. Moreover, I needed her.

I have never claimed to understand love. As newborn Rats, we love our Mother because her body provides warmth and food. Later we love our family members because they go upon risky adventures with us and because it's better having such connections than being alone.

None of that approached what I felt for Constanze. My feelings for her reached deep into a place I'd never even dreamed existed. She became my reason for living. I awoke in the morning because she was there, and I stole food to feed her rather than me. I spoke to her and engaged her to keep her from growing agitated and to keep the madness at bay.

In that, I fear I did not quite succeed.

She would rage in her sleep, as I say, rail at Elissabet and threaten to kill her. She spoke of some great injury that had been done to her and that I dared not broach with her during daylight. But I wondered.

Sometimes even during the day her eyes would turn mad and desperate, as they had that last afternoon back at the house. She would pace the cramped space of the shed and mutter dire complaints.

"It is not fair. I was taken from everything that makes me *me*. You do not understand, Marquell. You do not understand."

But I did. I too had been taken from my world, had lost everything.

Except her.

I could only wonder what had transpired at the house after we left. A search, without question. Pursuit. The constables, no doubt. Anger and tears for Timor and Elissabet respectively.

But what, after? Had the wedding gone forward? What of the dress and all our plans and preparations? I had been plucked once again from everything that was familiar to me.

We had no way of getting news there in the back of the shed. We were neither comfortable nor uncomfortable. In summer, it would have been sweltering, but we now slid into fall.

And then, all unexpectedly, I did get some news.

I'd been plundering the house pantry all this while for our food. I never took much. Half the time Constanze refused to eat, and I could exist on little. Still, over time it added up.

We used a back corner of the garden for our midden, and I took our daily water from the house cistern, having stolen a metal pot for the purpose. None of that could go undiscovered for long.

One afternoon while Constanze slept, I heard voices and crept around the bales of hay to peer out the crack in the shed door.

A Man I recognized stood talking with another younger Man on the back step of the house. His aggrieved words came to me.

"I don't understand it! Food has been going missing, I'm sure of it. Could someone be breaking in?"

"I don't see how," said the other Man, and I knew him by his voice. He too dwelt in the house. "The latch is always set."

"Then it must be rats."

"Impossible. All the rats are gone."

"Are they? So that wizard fellow claimed. What if they've come back?"

My blood turned cold. If the people of the household did a search for Rats, they could well discover our hiding place in the shed. Add to that the possibility—

"We should call that wizard fellow back," said one of the Men, voicing my worst fear. Timor here, with all his powers. Able to find me, to harm me.

Even more terrifying, able to harm Constanze, to rip her from my arms and lock her away.

"Whatever you do, don't tell your mother. If she thinks there are rats back on the premises, she'll go mad. Let me take care of it. I'll contact the constables first, see if there's any word of miscreants breaking in around here. Then take it to the Lord Mayor and that wizard."

"Not a word to Mother."

"But son, you could be right—the rats may indeed be back."

No, they were leaving.

Chapter Twenty-Two

"Gather up your things, Constanze. We are leaving this place."

Constanze opened her eyes to slits and peered up at me from the straw bed. Some days she slept too much and most nights far too little. Part of her illness, I supposed.

That she was ill, I had no doubt. She'd always been pale. Now her skin had taken on a pasty quality. Her hair had gone dull and become tangled. Her eyes either stared blankly or glittered with feverish distress. She'd wasted away to little more than bones covered by skin.

It occurred to me I'd done her few favors by bringing her away. True, she was not in a cell at the asylum, but pent up here in this dim shed was scarcely better.

"Leaving? Why?"

"It is no longer safe for us here. I have heard the Men talking."

"Men? What men?"

"Men of the house. They know I've been stealing food. If they summon Timor—"

We stared into one another's eyes with identical terror. "All right," she said breathlessly. "I don't have much." Her blanket which we now shared, spread over the straw. A shawl. A comb she never employed. "Where will we go?"

I didn't know. Somewhere around the town. So long as no one glimpsed us.

"Constanze?"

"Yes?"

"Do you truly think Timor will hunt us down?"

She considered it. I seemed to have caught her in a lucid moment, startled out of her gloom by my announcement.

"Yes. He is a small man at heart. A very small man. We have upset Elissabet, and for that he will insist on revenge. He never considers others." She paused to cup my cheek. "Not like you."

"It will be dark soon. We will move out then."

"I trust you, Marquell. I will follow you."

A lot of responsibility to carry, for an accidental Man who would be a Rat.

****

A terrible time followed. The weather turned foul, as it so often did with the arrival of autumn. Rain blew in from the sea.

With no set place to settle, we were frequently wet and cold. The hidey holes and caches I'd known as a Rat no longer fit me. Eyes watched from everywhere—it seemed we seldom went unobserved. So sharp was my fear of pursuit and discovery, I imagined danger at every hand. Or perhaps the peril truly did exist.

For I agreed with Constanze. Timor would not let this rest. I had left him high and dry a day before an event I'd been supposed to carry, in large part. He had the ultimate power of revenge against me—he had only to refuse to turn me back into what I truly was.

I thought about it when I should be sleeping. The rest of the time I focused on Constanze and keeping her safe. It is one thing, hiding when you are the size of a Rat. Quite another now. Just as it is easier stealing Rat-sized crumbs of food rather than enough to keep two Men alive.

No question I was worried. Perhaps that is what precipitated the disaster that followed. Or perhaps I was worried because I had a presentiment of what was to come.

We were staying in the rear porch of an empty house. We'd been there two days, and already I thought about moving on, since neighbors might see me coming and going and become suspicious. We were ragged by then, and as most property owners were house-proud, we were all too apt to garner notice.

I left Constanze sleeping in the afternoon and went out to find food. I remember whispering to her before I left, "Stay here and keep quiet. I will be back soon." I don't know if she heard me, but I think so, for her eyelashes twitched.

I stole a last look at her as I slipped out. Did I sense I might never see her again?

I straightened my coat as best I could and walked to the market area a couple of streets away. It had been several days since we'd had food, and my stomach complained to me. There was a baker who put his wares out front. I'd taken to lifting a loaf from him every day or so. I told myself that was all I needed—one loaf to keep us. Just thinking about the aroma of it and the firm crust made my mouth water.

Two attributes make Rats good thieves—we are determined and will work a long time, chewing through a wall, for a morsel. And we are fast on the getaway.

I was not fast enough this time.

Using my customary method, I bypassed the stall in front of the bakery at close range, snagging a loaf as I did so. I never looked at my target or looked back. I always shoved the loaf beneath the hem of my coat and kept walking.

On this afternoon, however, I heard a cry. "You there! Stop, thief! Constables! It's the thief who's been stealing all my bread!"

Constables? I went cold with horror and risked one look back. The owner of the shop stood in the doorway, his face red with anger, and a phalanx of policemen emerged from around the side of the building.

I have no idea why they were there, if it were bad luck or planning. The latter, I suspect. I had gone once too often to the same pantry, so to speak.

I ran, prodded by instinct. In my life as a Rat I'd run from Cats my share of times. This was very like. The constables knew the streets and spread out, one of them constantly blowing his whistle so passersby would get out of the way. Some passersby, on sheer principle, got into the act and tried to block my path, making me duck around them. I dodged, I cut down alleys, I ran until I thought my lungs would burst. I lost the prize somewhere along the route, dropping it in a gutter. My one thought was of returning to Constanze, but I could not lead them to her.

In the end a citizen—a younger Man—stepped out and tripped me. I fell, rolled, and skinned my hands on the cobbles. I never had a chance to get up. The lead constable—he with the ear-splitting whistle—was on me far too quickly and hauled me up.

He must have been twice my size. I have mentioned I was not big for a Man. Lean and wiry, my only remaining strength lay in desperation.

I tried to wriggle my way free from his grip, but his fellows and half the residents of the street steamed up and surrounded us.

Trapped.

The constables hit me with their batons and the observers looked on with interest. I bared my teeth, the Rat's instinctive reaction at being cornered.

The constables were all as badly out of breath as I. The shop owner, who had somehow kept pace with the chase, stepped up and said, "He's the thief keeps stealing from my stall."

I hoped the whole bakery was being picked over in his absence.

Staunchly I sought to deny the charge. "I've stolen nothing."

"No?" he snarled. "What about that loaf you dropped back there?"

I held up my hands, both of them bloodied. "I had no loaf."

"Only because you dropped it!" he howled.

The lead constable shook me as a terrier might a Rat. "Is this so?"

"No!" I maintained.

"Half the street saw you carrying that loaf."

My thoughts seethed. I had to get back to Constanze. What would she think, what would she do if I failed to return? Could she survive without me?

The urgency of it made my head go light. I struggled anew in the constable's grip. One of his fellows stepped in to help hold me.

"Wait a moment!" cried someone from the crowd. "I know this fellow."

A well-dressed middle-aged Man stepped forward, eyeing me closely where I hung in the grip of the officers. "Aren't you the wizard's man?"

My heart seemed to seize in my chest before falling so hard, I thought I'd surely die.

"No."

"Wizard?" questioned the lead constable, ignoring me.

"Of course you are. I saw you in his company when he did that job for the Lord Mayor." His expression sharpened. "He's been looking high and low for you. Constable, surely you're aware of this? Master Springerle's servant skipped out on him. Master Springerle is anxious to get him back again."

"Probably stole from his household as well." The constable shook me slightly.

"I did not," I said it more loudly. "You're mistaken. I never met any wizard."

"I wouldn't forget a man of your singular appearance. And look, he's still wearing his livery jacket."

"So he is." The constable who held me said to another, "You know where this wizard fellow lives?"

"Garten Street, ain't it? He's the one lodging at Master Carp's house."

"Run and fetch him, then."

"I believe," said the dratted Man who'd recognized me, "there is a reward for his return."

The constable ran.

I wanted to disappear where I stood, slink away, run away, dematerialize—whatever it took to keep from facing Timor again. What would he do to me? Have me charged? Toss me into a cell? For what? I'd taken

162

nothing—save Constanze.

Oh, I was in deep, dire trouble. Whatever else happened I couldn't betray Constanze's whereabouts. No matter what Timor did to me.

How could I protect her, though, if I'd been captured? And what would she do when I failed to return?

Chapter Twenty-Three

It did not take long for Timor to arrive. I stood all the while in the late afternoon sun, sweating as only a Man can do, and worrying. The constables never loosened their grips on me. Believe me, I was waiting for just one opportunity to be away, to scamper. If they followed me, I'd lead them on a merry dance through the town, as only a Rat could, rather than take them back to Constanze.

But oh, the better part of my worry centered upon her. I cared little enough what might happen to me in comparison. I imagined her waiting and waiting for me. She was used to me making brief forays out for what we needed. She would starve on her own. Else she would emerge and be caught in turn.

Timor arrived in a carriage, accompanied by the constable. He emerged wearing his good black coat—the one I had brushed for him so often—looking haughty and important. Those waiting hustled around him, and the remaining constables hauled me up.

Timor also looked angry, as I discovered when he shot a look at me. You must remember I'd seen him in all sorts of moods—at ease with Elissabet, dignified with officials of the town, annoyed and angry. When he worked his magic, he got a certain expression in his bi-colored eyes. They glowed with power.

I feared that look most of all.

Now he fixed me with a fierce stare. The brown eye appeared cold and hard, glittering. The green one gleamed as the magic within him burned. Corresponding heat and cold drenched me.

"Master Springerle," cried the head constable who held me, "is this your man?"

"It is." Timor responded with a heavy tone that hovered between rage and satisfaction. "Where did you find him?"

"Thieving, Master." The baker stepped forward, his fleshy face flushed. "He stole a loaf from me."

"Ah." Something glittered in Timor's eyes. "Back to your old ways, eh, Marquell?"

I said nothing. I'm not sure I still possessed the power of speech.

Timor stepped closer to me, and I could feel the magic in him. I swear I could. "I've been looking for you—you and Constanze. You've caused me a lot of trouble."

"Master Springerle," the baker interrupted, "is it true there's a reward set for this fellow's capture?"

Timor glared at him, and it was a relief to be released from his gaze, even if only for a moment. "Yes."

"It was I who first spotted him," the baker declared. "I believe he's been thieving from my shop regular, so you might say I'm owed."

"Oh? Is that what you think?"

"And," the constable who had hold of me took it up, "we three apprehended him."

"You shall all get what you deserve," Timor declared. "As shall he." He fixed me with those pied eyes once more.

165

The head constable grunted. "Then I'll take him in, shall I? Lock him up for thievery as charged."

Timor ignored him. He now stood so close to me our toes might have touched had I been on my own feet. He scanned my face and demanded, "Where is she?"

Constanze, he meant. He wanted revenge upon me, yes, but that was nothing to what he wanted from her. For she had upset Elissabet, and to him that was an unforgivable violation.

I could not betray Constanze, no matter what Timor did.

"Tell me, Marquell." His green eye began to glow more brightly. "You ran off with her, didn't you? You helped her escape me."

I shook my head.

"Don't lie." His voice turned to iron. "You know what will happen if you do."

The crowd listened to this avidly. They knew something more than a mere apprehension took place, though they did not understand what.

Can you imagine how I felt? Cornered. Trapped. It is a Rat's instinct to flee, to run, and despite my form, I may never have been more a Rat than at that moment.

Employing strength I didn't know I possessed, I broke free from the Man who held me. As a Rat might, I scrambled over feet, pushing bodies aside. If only I could get away, I could lose them, disappear into the town. Eventually find my way back to Constanze.

The crowd exclaimed. They made way for the constables' pursuit, but it wasn't needed. Something hit me in the back of the head. It felt like a rock, but I think it was magic—a bolt of magic hard as iron.

I fell to the cobbles and knew no more.

****

Constanze.

I came to my senses with her name on my lips and a frantic leap of the heart. I swear she was the very first thing of which I thought. Pain exploded an instant later, starting at the back of my head and radiating through me, enough to steal my breath.

I pried my eyelids open one at a time. Not comprehending what I saw—blurry and confusing—my eyes closed again.

"Where is she?"

The voice, relentless, had my eyes opening again and my brain trying to make sense of things that—well, made no sense.

I lay—or rather crouched—half on my side with both hands braced against the floor. I seemed to be surrounded by a number of vertical lines. They glowed softly—or perhaps were just fuzzy due to my confused perspective. Beyond them, I could dimly glimpse a room. And there…

I blinked desperately, not liking what I saw.

I was in a cage. The lines I saw were the bars, so close to my face they blurred, for the cage was very small. Barely large enough for me to pick up my head and certainly not long enough for me to stretch my limbs.

Horror suffused me, so strong it nearly beat back the pain. I have said how a Rat dreads being trapped. This brought on a Rat's panic, visceral and strong.

I was, though, still a Man. I could see my hands braced against the floor, and I wore my clothing, now all scuffed and dirty.

Fighting the panic, I peered beyond the bars and

saw—Timor.

The wizard lounged on a chaise just beyond the bars of my cage. I recognized the piece of furniture as being in the rear parlor of the house where we'd lived. He'd taken me there, then.

Though he appeared at his ease, he was not. I sensed the tension coiled inside him, and even through the bars I could see the way his eyes glowed—especially the green one.

"Where is she?" he greeted me, and I wondered if I'd said her name—Constanze—aloud.

I tried to sit up, and the bars overhead smacked my skull. Pain radiated through me more brightly. The cage was very, very small.

"Let me out."

"Oh, I will, Marquell. I will. Just as soon as you tell me Constanze's whereabouts. Lead me to her, and you will go free."

I could not do that. Constanze, weakened and fragile, would never endure his wrath.

"I cannot do that," I said aloud, gasping it through the pain.

"Why not? Why would you sacrifice yourself for her?"

Because I love her. I did not say that aloud. I'd only just recognized it in full, and as knowledge, it was far too precious to share. Yes, Rats are capable of love. And yes, we value the emotion, if only because it comes to us so rarely.

Timor's pied gaze burned at me. "Let me clarify your position, Marquell. That cage you are in—it is a magical one, created by me. No ordinary cage, you understand. The bars have the power to bind and burn.

You will note it is not very large. Every time you defy me it will grow smaller. The bars will close upon you, and it will cause great pain. A terrible situation for anyone—rat or human—to find himself, you would agree."

I would.

"But you have only to lead me to Constanze, and I will release you. I'll even change you back to a rat, if that's what you wish. Just as I promised."

Trapped. I was trapped. Just like a Rat in a net, unable to bite his way free. Scramble as I might, the net would only close more tightly.

"Is that what you want?" His hard voice prodded at me. "To be a rat?"

It was. It had been all along. At this moment I wanted nothing so much as to be free of the trap. Well, I wanted one thing more.

I said nothing, my teeth bared from the pain of it.

"Let me tell you what has happened since you left," he said, still with that falsely casual air. "After Constanze ruined Elissabet's wedding dress, my darling fiancée had a breakdown. Inconsolable, she was, and I with no way to make things better for her."

"Constanze did not ruin the wedding dress. Why would she? She worked countless hours over it. Berta spilled the tea—"

"And Constanze reacted as no servant—as no friend—ever should. We treated you like friends, you will agree with that. And perhaps it was our greatest mistake. But my dear Elissabet has no one else. She's been close to Constanze a long time. She wants her back and is in fact distraught still, without her."

"She wants her back—so you can abuse her?"

"No. When have we ever done that?"

I might outline all of it, the many injustices and Constanze's deep resentment. He would not see it. He saw nothing wrong, in fact, with using others to his benefit.

I was not even a person to him, I was a Rat, and he would crush me as casually as the Men who stomped my kind with their great boots.

"Please," I said, "let it go."

"Don't you mean, 'Let me go'?" He got to his feet, still behaving casually, but there was nothing casual about it.

"The wedding," he told me, "did not take place. Oh, everything was set. The guests showed up. The decorations were resplendent. At the last minute, Elissabet was too distraught to go through with the ceremony. As a consequence, she is not yet mine. She wants Constanze back, and she will have what she wants. Do you understand?"

He raised his hand and made a gesture with his fingers. The bars around me contracted. Where they made contact with my body, they burned.

Pain exploded like bright light before everything went dark again.

Chapter Twenty-Four

I awoke wondering where I was, who I was. For an instant before I opened my eyes, I thought I was back in Mother's nest in the wall, dark, close, and safe, with the furry bodies of my littermates pressed in all around me.

Something did press against me. I stirred, and the pain struck deep. The cage—I lay still trapped in Timor's hands.

"Have you ever noticed," a voice asked almost idly, "how like a rat your servant looks? Those sharp features and those beady eyes."

"Do tell," another voice drawled—Timor. Timor and Elissabet, they were sitting at their ease in the back parlor, watching me suffer.

I pried my eyes open farther to look at them.

Elissabet sat on the chaise longue he'd occupied last time, her slippered feet in the air and her ruffled petticoats on display. She looked both amused and petulant, but her eyes widened when she saw I'd come awake.

"At last. Now perhaps we will get somewhere."

Timor leaned on the back of the chaise behind her. He sent a hard look of warning at me.

I ignored it. "Let me go," I snarled and bared my teeth.

"There!" Elissabet pointed at me. "Does he not look exactly like a rat?"

"By my soul," Timor drawled, "he does. Odd I never noticed."

Elissabet shivered. "Hideous creature. Make him tell me where she is."

She. Constanze. My heart leaped at the very thought of her.

"Just ask him," Timor told her.

She made a moue of disgust. "Must I?"

"Ask him," Timor reiterated.

"Where is Constanze?"

My voice ground its way up from my belly, half smothered by pain. "I don't know." It was true. How much time had passed since I'd been captured in the town? She might still be where I'd left her. She might have grown tired of waiting for me and left.

"But"—Elissabet tipped her head—"you did help her escape from here. From me."

"The truth, now." Timor flexed his fingers, and the bars of the cage collapsed still farther around my body. I gasped.

"Answer Mistress Elissabet," Timor instructed.

"Yes."

"Yes, what?"

"Yes, I helped her escape you. She did no wrong. She had done all you asked."

"She turned into a madwoman! She might have flown at me." Elissabet's face crumpled. "She who was supposed to be closest to me in all the world. She must pay for that."

"She has paid." Fighting the pain that enfolded me, I sought to reason with Elissabet. She'd seemed almost kind at times in the past. Maybe I could tap that softness now. "She's been terribly ill since we left, and weak. Locking her up would kill her. You know it."

A curious look came to Elissabet's face, half grief and half satisfaction. It was as if she played a role and would not show what she truly felt.

Perhaps she'd always played a role. Maybe beneath it all she was as cruel as Timor.

Maybe Constanze had always been right about her.

"Still," she said petulantly, "Her madness threatens me, doesn't it? Mad people must be locked away for the good of everyone."

"Or you could be merciful. Be merciful, Mistress Elissabet, and let her go."

"She ruined my wedding. Did Timor tell you I could not go through with it? I just couldn't face it, after that."

"I'm sorry." I gasped. It felt as if the bars burned through the clothing I wore and into my body.

"I want her back with me so I might decide what becomes of her. She belongs to me."

"She doesn't."

"She does, in ways you cannot begin to understand. Tell him, Timor."

"Constanze may not be entirely what you think, Marquell," Timor said.

My mind raced, or tried to. Thought of any kind was imminently difficult beneath the weight of the pain.

"If you care anything about her, you'll let her go." Even as I spoke the words, I recognized their futility. Elissabet cared for no one but herself. Not the cost to others, not their misery or pain. As selfish as Timor, the two of them deserved each other.

"If she cared anything about me, she never would have reacted the way she did. She knew how important that wedding was to me."

Not too important, if she'd not gone through with it.

Elissabet leaned over me and cried, "Tell me where she is."

I could not. I would not. Even though it hurt to do so, I shook my head.

Elissabet's eyes glowed with rage. She turned to Timor. "Torture him or do whatever you must. Just make him talk."

****

An incalculable amount of time later, Elissabet flounced from the parlor in frustration, angry tears on her face. I'd been in and out of consciousness. I'd moaned, I'd begged, though I regret having to admit it. I'd squealed like the Rat I was.

The one thing I had not done was give Elissabet what she wanted.

So lost in pain was I that my success in withholding the information provided me very little satisfaction. I acted as I did to protect Constanze, not to thwart Elissabet.

What is love? Is it in fact a selfish emotion? Did loving Constanze make me every bit as selfish as Elissabet? As Timor? Because I needed Constanze. I needed her happy—not locked away somewhere and driven to madness, but bright and aware, supplying a lack in my life.

I needed to feel the way I did when she was near me. And that frightened me almost more than the movements of Timor's fingers.

Rats by and large live independent lives. We are aware of each other. We play and mate and even share.

I missed everyone I'd lost, but not the way I missed Constanze, even after one day away from her.

Need, yes. Selfish need.

Timor strolled up to the cage, where I lay exhausted by my suffering, and toed the bars. I did not move even though the toe of his boot was a mere breath from my nose. If he meant to kick me, he would. Nothing I could do would prevent it.

Instead he said, "Give it up, Marquell. Why would you insist on continuing to protect her?"

I looked up at him and saw his expression turn sly and knowing. "Never tell me you're in love with the chit? With that poor pallid specimen who has nothing but anger to recommend her?"

I said nothing.

He leaned over me. Neither of his eyes glowed, now. He looked calm.

I knew that to be deceptive. He was hard and cruel, anything but calm.

"So you fell in love with my lady's maid," he said, emphasizing the final word in the strangest fashion. "How ironic! Does she love you too? A better question—" He forestalled my answer. "Does she know what you are?"

Feebly, I shook my head.

"Ah, Marquell, what do you think she would say? What if she learned she'd run off in fact with a filthy rat?"

"I am not filthy," I gasped.

"Women"—he gave a queer little laugh—"women such as Constanze consider all rats filthy. Why do you think the women of Regis Towne persuaded their men to hire me, why they wanted your kind dead? Women scream and screech and flee when they see your kind. Is Constanze any different?"

I did not know. I didn't even know if she loved me the way I loved her. She'd been kind to me. She'd kissed me.

Would she kiss a Rat?

"Believe me, Marquell, a future between the two of you is out of the question. There is no hope. Why not let me give you what you've wanted from the first? I will free you from the cruel trap wherein you lie. You lead me to Constanze, and I will transform you back into a rat. Just as I promised. You need not concern yourself with what happens to Constanze thereafter."

I could not trust him.

"You know," he mused, "you mustn't worry about Constanze. Elissabet is very angry with her, it's true. But she's actually quite fond of Constanze. I don't think she will hurt her much. Just enough to teach her a lesson about defiance."

I did not believe a word of it.

"Things will just go back to the way they were." He waved his hand, and I flinched. "Before you came."

I watched his fingers and said nothing.

"On the other hand," he leaned still closer, so I stared directly into his pied eyes, "I could tell Constanze the truth of what you actually are."

"You'd need to find her first."

"I will. It will take longer than if you lead me to her. But she will have to come out of hiding eventually. She will need food. Water. Lead me to her, Marquell, for her sake if nothing else. If you do not, I will leave you in that cage. When I find Constanze, I will bring her here and transform you before her eyes."

Not that, no!

"On the other hand, if you agree to lead me to her, I will keep you out of her sight, transform you back into a rat, and set you free. You may scuttle away back to your old life."

Could I? Never. But he did not need to know that. I raised my cheek from the floor, the better to stare him in the eye.

"Very well, you have beaten me. I agree. I will lead you to Constanze."

Chapter Twenty-Five

You may say I'm a fool, and yes, I would agree that is true. I've done many foolish things in my life, none more so perhaps than falling in love with Constanze, she a female Man and I a Rat. There was never truly any hope in it.

And it was foolish, yes, to make a deal of any sort with Timor. But I believed deep in my heart that if only I could get out of that infernal torturous cage, I could escape him and make my way back to Constanze.

What might happen then, I had no idea. I did not look so far ahead.

Timor was right—he could have eyes watching everywhere in the town, even if he relied only upon the constables.

Instinct told me that like any Rat I could dodge and wriggle and scramble my way out. And instinct wanted to take me back to Constanze.

If she found out the truth about me, if he forced her to watch as he transformed me from an erstwhile house steward back into a furry rodent, I would then have to see her recoil from me in horror. After that I would care little what happened to me. I might take myself, in the form of a Rat, to the Lord Mayor so the authorities would know Timor had not done the job for which he'd been paid.

I hoped it would not come to that. I saw myself

giving Timor the slip somewhere in town and returning to the place Constanze and I had been, still in my current form.

And if that meant I would never be turned back into a Rat?

I did not want to think about it. One step at a time. First of all, get out of the cage.

I failed to consider my physical state after many hours of torture. When Timor dissolved the bars of the cage with a gesture and a ponderous frown of effort, I found I could not rise, and I lay there panting like a Rat that has been chased down by terriers.

With a look of profound distaste, Timor hauled me up, using the back of my coat.

Elissabet tiptoed back into the room, her eyes wide. "You are letting him go?"

"No. He has agreed to lead me to Constanze. Haven't you, Marquell?"

"Yes, Master Timor."

Elissabet's face lit. "You're going after her now?"

"We are."

"I want to come."

I straightened where I stood. This could be a good or a bad thing. Another set of eyes for me to dodge or a distraction for Timor.

"Nay," he told her. "Things may get rough out there."

"Rough?"

He lifted his eyebrows.

She said, "Oh. Magic?"

"Maybe. You wait here, my love. I will bring her to you."

"Good." She crossed her arms. "Then there will be

a reckoning."

"Elissabet," Timor said with a glance at me, "you know you will treat Constanze kindly. Is she not your oldest friend?"

"Indeed." Elissabet wrinkled her forehead. "Just bring her back, mind. She—she is very important to me."

****

Out in the street, I struggled to determine how much time had elapsed while I remained inside. Evening fell swiftly. I could only think it an advantage to me. I knew the shadows of this town and how to make the most of them. I need only slip my chain.

Not that Timor chained me, in actual fact, but he walked a step behind me with his hand upon my shoulder. And I swear I could feel his power in that touch, just waiting to be unleashed.

Did I fear him? I am not ashamed to say I did—on Constanze's behalf even more than my own. Though I would not be surprised if I lost my life this night.

"Lead me," Timor said. "And do not make me call the constables."

I drew upon the last of my strength. Not much remained. I thought of Constanze lying on the abandoned porch where I'd left her and turned in the opposite direction.

"This way?" He squeezed my shoulder in warning. "Are you sure?"

"We have been hiding out on the waterfront."

"Ah. Go on, then."

How long could I lead him awry before he grew suspicious?

Usually the waterfront teemed with activity. Now,

however, the day workers had cleared off. The only light to split the gloom spilled from the various taverns.

The water lapped dark and mysterious against the stone pier, and I shivered. It had been a mistake to come here. I could hear again the scrabbling of feet on the stones, the splash of furry bodies hitting the water. The desperate paddling as every Rat I knew swam to its death.

Wholly spooked, I stopped and faced the water. If only I could cause Timor to jump in there, that I might be rid of him. But I had no such power. And if he went to his death, I would never be a Rat—my true self—again.

"I think you are playing with me," he said in a voice like death. "We had a deal. You need to fulfill it."

I turned and faced him. It had not been a good day. My body still hurt from the agonies it had endured, and I felt dangerously depleted. Worse, my worry for Constanze chewed at me constantly. But whatever my form, I was still part Rat. Rats are tough.

I might possess a measure of magic, after all, in my love for Constance. It made me care more for her than for myself.

It gave me the courage to face off against a powerful wizard.

I was afraid of him—make no mistake. A frightened Rat will run. If he cannot run, he will stand and fight.

"I will not be leading you to her," I told him. "Not for anything."

His brow wrinkled. "Careful, Marquell. Those who break promises to me pay a heavy price. I hold all power over you. Put a foot wrong, and you will never again be a Rat. That is what you want, is it not? To be a Rat once more."

Was it? Yes. My very being ached for the familiar, for the scents, sights, and perspectives of the Rat world. But I thought of Constanze. Not of Constanze as I'd left her, so pale and ill, but of Constanze as I'd come to know her—kind and brisk and accepting of me despite my appearance. I thought of countless days spent working with her in the kitchen, of words shared, and smiles. I thought of afternoons at the shops, of sitting on the back stoop with her gazing at the stars. Of feeling comfortable with her as I'd never been with anyone else, and of holding her in my arms.

Life, I suddenly saw, was made of such moments. And, Rat or no, I would fight for them.

Timor's green eye began to glow. "You will not defeat me," he said as if reading my thoughts. "You cannot win."

"Perhaps not."

"Run," he said, "and I will snare you with my magic. I promise you"—he gestured at the sea behind me—"you shall end like all your fellows."

"Better that," I told him, "than to betray one I love."

"Love?" He scoffed at it. "You? A rat? What if I transform you back now? Will your Constanze want you?"

Perhaps not. Indeed, for all my wondering, I didn't know what Constanze would do if she beheld me in my true form. Run from me screaming, as he said? I wouldn't be able to tell her who I was. She would have no way of knowing.

But there comes a time when a Man or a Rat must

find his own power.

"Do what you will," I told Timor, and baring my teeth, I leaped.

He did not expect it. I am certain the only thing that saved me was that I took him unawares. He had no time to cast a spell. I leaped for his throat, closing my hands upon it like claws, and so he had no opportunity to make a deadly gesture. For he used his hands to try and pluck mine off him, instead.

We thrashed, we struggled and rolled across the stones. I could feel his strength. He was much bigger than I was, even as a Man. But I had the desperation of a cornered Rat on my side.

Every time he tried to flex his fingers to cast a spell, I bit them. I could feel the magic building up inside him and knew I couldn't let it escape. It would scald, it would annihilate me. So when he began to mutter words, I bit at his face also.

A terrible thing it would have been, to observe. But there was no one there to see, and the elemental struggle continued across the stones and onto the pier.

He tried to dash my head against the stones. My senses swam, but I held on, thrashing and struggling to become uppermost. I never realized how close we were to the edge until we went over and the water took us, still entwined in a dark and deadly embrace.

The shock of it almost made me let go of him, but I knew if I did—if I let him use his powers—I was finished. We sank like two stones, and instinctive horror suffused me.

With my eyes wide, I could see the water was murky, full of shapes that, in the darkness of it, I could not identify. They might have been anything—lost cargo from the docks, stones, wrecks, parts of the pier itself. But I believed they were the bodies of my kin, those lost close to shore.

I was in a graveyard.

That conviction lent me fight. I kicked frantically with my feet. We sank still.

Rats have an instinctive fear of water, but we can swim—at least till our strength gives out. I had little chance, though, weighted with a wizard who seemed to have gone rigid in my hands. Timor did not kick. He did not fight to save himself. He seemed petrified.

I could not hold on to him if I wanted to live. Neither could I let go of him if I feared his magic.

I might finish him, if I took him down with me. Or I might live for Constanze's sake.

Chapter Twenty-Six

The dark water filled my ears and went up my nose. It felt oily and stank of muck and fish and all the things that had gone into it. It tasted of salt and seaweed. I could no longer see Timor's face for the gloom. He'd now gone utterly limp in my hands.

When I felt the silt of the harbor bottom beneath my feet, I let go of him. At the demand of my lungs, I launched myself upward and broke the surface of the water.

There I hovered, gasping. From my present perspective the stone pier looked high and unscalable. I could spy no hand or foothold.

The day Timor murdered all the Rats, I had not seen any of them try to jump back on land. They'd been driven by enchantment, to be sure. They'd had little chance to look back. I now flailed in the oily water, eyes searching for some purchase. I could feel my weakness increase by the moment. The torture back at the house and the struggle in the past moments had drained me. I had not much left.

And if I were to die here like all my fellows, would that not be fitting? My weary body dragged at me, urging me to give up.

Yet I needed to reach Constanze. She would be waiting, helpless, for my return. I must get back to her. Love demanded it.

My desperate gaze found it then, barely visible in the dark—a place where the wall had crumbled. There might be a handhold.

I splashed my way over to it and, expending the last of my strength, pulled myself up and out. I lay on the damp stones of the pier, making them wetter, and just breathed.

My heart pounded in my ears, and I thought for that one moment I was free. I need only gather my strength enough to scramble up and find my way to where I'd left Constanze.

Staggering, I got to my feet. I could hear the water lapping against the pier and faint music from the nearest tavern.

Nothing—not so much as a gurgle—more.

I started away. One step, two. A great splash sounded behind me.

"Marquell! Marquell!"

Dread washed over me like a jet of icy rain. I turned around slowly and saw him there in the black water, floundering and struggling to stay above the surface.

"Marquell! Pull me out."

Oh, by the sweet god of all the Rats, what was I to do?

He splashed his way over to the pier, but he had not seen the handholds I'd used. And like me, he was spent.

"Marquell? Is there a way up?"

I could leave him there to die. The thought occurred to me quite clearly as I stood watching him struggle to stay afloat. One might say he deserved it, and there was a fabulous irony in the fact that he would die the same way as so many of his victims.

Clearly, he could not swim. As I watched, he went down once, only to flail his way up again, gasping.

If I stood here and did nothing, it would not take long.

"Marquell! Please, I can't swim."

I walked to the edge of the pier and gazed down at him. Even in the dark his face shone pale, and his expression showed his desperation.

"Why?" I called back to him. "Why should I help you?"

"If you don't, I cannot change you back into a rat. You will be doomed to remain a man forever."

There was that. Could I live with it?

"Pull me out," he beseeched, "and I will make you a rich man. You shall have the contents of my pockets. And a spell for good fortune."

I hunkered down at the edge of the pier, my hands dangling. He leaped for one of them and missed. "Marquell, please. Pull me out, and I will change you back at once. Whatever you ask!"

"How do I know I can trust you?"

"I swear it on my life! Should I go back on my word, may every ill fortune befall me."

"If I haul you out, if I save you, you will agree to whatever I want?"

"Yes. Yes!"

He went under for the third time. Throwing myself onto my belly and reaching down, I managed to snag the back of his coat and retrieve him.

I would like to think I did it out of the goodness of my heart, that despite being a Rat I was a better Man than he. In all honesty, I thought of Constanze yet, what

I might take to her, what I might do for her. So I can make no such lofty claims.

It took the last of my strength to haul him out of the water. Had he raised a hand against me then, I would have had no defense. But he was as spent as I.

We lay there like comrades rather than enemies, both soaked and trying to recover ourselves. Eventually I picked myself up and looked at him.

He now bore little resemblance to the cunning, conceited Man I'd first met. His coat was ruined, his fine boots seeped water. His hair lay plastered to his head like seaweed. His confidence—indeed his arrogance—was flown.

I gasped the words, "If you try to cheat me, I will throw you back in." An idle threat; I doubted I had the strength.

"I will not cheat you. Only let me catch my breath."

He caught his, and I caught mine. I began to realize I'd escaped the same cruel fate as all my fellows, even if I'd perhaps failed to give them justice.

At last he struggled to a sitting position and said, "If you wish me to turn you back into a rat, I will. But you will have to allow me a whiskey first—and time to regain my powers."

"I do not want you to turn me back into a Rat."

He stared. I did not blame him, I could myself scarce believe it.

He blinked a few times. "Might I ask why?"

I'd been thinking about it. "How can I be with Constanze if I am not a Man?"

"So it's all about love, is it?" He began to laugh, softly at first and then so hard water came out of his mouth and nose.

"Is it humorous?" I asked, miffed.

"It is both humorous and ironic, though you will not understand why, and I am not about to tell you."

I glared at him.

"Do not worry, Marquell. I will fulfill my promise. It seems we are far too much alike for me to countenance doing you wrong."

Chapter Twenty-Seven

I made my way back to Constanze with my pockets stuffed full of gold and a wee spell or two I would be able to use in the future. At our parting, Timor said he never wanted to see me again, but he did clasp my hand and add that I had his gratitude for life.

Whatever that life might hold.

Constanze was up out of her bed, on her feet, and pacing frantically when I reached her. She came flying into my arms.

"Marquell! Oh, Marquell, where have you been? I was so worried and didn't know what to do."

"Hush, I am here now." I clutched her tight.

"You are all wet."

"I have been in the sea."

"You have? Why?"

"It doesn't matter now. Nothing does, so long as we are together."

She drew away just far enough to study my face. "I'm sorry."

"For what?"

"For being selfish and thinking only of my own anger and resentment. While you were gone I realized how unfair I've been. You did all you could to help me, and I thought only of the wrongs that had been done to me."

"We all have such thoughts."

"But I did not consider the great gift I'd been given. You, Marquell. Whatever I've been asked to sacrifice in the past, and whatever harm has been done to me, you more than make up for it."

I gazed into her eyes, wondering if I owed her the truth. She should know what I was. But Timor might be right. It could change how she felt about me.

"I want to spend the rest of my life with you," I told her.

"I would like that too, Marquell."

"But—"

"But—"

We both spoke the word at the same instant. A dull flush rose to her cheeks. "There is something I must tell you," she concluded.

"There is something I need to tell you also, Constanze. About me. I should have admitted it long ago when we began to grow close."

"Me first, before I lose my courage." She caught hold of my hands and towed me to the bed. "I could think of nothing else while you were gone. Let me say it now."

"Very well." Whatever she said, I thought, could not be worse than what I had to tell.

"Marquell, I love you. More—more than I ever thought to love anyone."

"I love you also."

"But I am not what you think me. You see before you a woman. Small perhaps, but utterly human. Yes?"

I nodded.

"Marquell, I am not a woman. It is a lie, an enchantment. I am a—a fairy. Timor changed me to this form. Since early childhood, I have been Elissabet's captive, forced to stay with her. When she decided to run away with Timor, he told her she could not take me unless I appeared human. So he—he—"

"Changed you?" I asked in disbelief.

"Yes."

I did not know what to say. I am sure my mouth hung open. "You say she forced you to stay with her?"

"Yes. Like a pet. Elissabet's father first captured me in a net when I was terribly small. Snatched from my family and never allowed to go back to them. They pierced my wings so I could not fly." Two tears trickled down her cheeks. "I amused Elissabet, and she grew attached. But I suffered terribly. At least where we lived while she remained home, I still had the trees all around me. And the clean air. I could smell my home, even if I was not allowed to return there."

The cruelty of it struck at me, the sheer selfishness. The things Men do to please themselves!

Misreading my appalled expression, she quavered, "There—I knew you would be disgusted and repelled, finding out I am not human. That I am something other—a fairy. I suspected you would no longer want to be near me." Her pale eyes searched mine before she confessed, "Timor said always he would change me back when Elissabet needed me no longer. But she always needed me. I thought at least I might return home, even if I could no longer fly. Then I met you, and I thought if I remained human we might be together."

So this was why Timor had laughed there at the end. Ah, but the joke was on him.

Tenderly, I caught her face between my palms. "I have something to tell you also." And I did. Heart pounding high and hard in my chest, I explained how Grandfather and I had been caught at the back of the spell that had enchanted all the Rats of Regis Towne. I told her why Timor had forced me to remain a Man for a time.

"He promised he'd change me back too," I told her as I concluded the accounting. "He deceived both of us."

"So he did. Promises, it seems, are easy for Men to make and hard for them to keep."

"So you see, Constanze, I am a Rat. Not the Man you supposed. Does it make a difference to you? Will it make you turn away from me?"

For answer, she pressed her lips to mine. The kiss was sweet and full of devotion. When it ended, she whispered, "It was never your coat I liked so much as the beautiful spirit inside it. You are one of the kindest and gentlest beings I have ever known."

"And you are one of the most constant. Will it break your heart to stay with me and never be a fairy again?"

"With my heart in your keeping, it can never break. Love, it seems, requires sacrifice."

"So it does."

"If I give up being a fairy and you give up being a rat, if we meet in the middle, we can stay together." She rested her head upon my breast. "And that's a gift I won't refuse."

****

We left the town soon after, with a load of goods on my back and some of Timor's gold spent. Taking our time, for both of us were still weak, we walked away. It took us days, but we reached the forest where we'd gone that one Sunday afternoon, and eventually we found a cottage and began a life there. A new life for both of us.

I will not say that neither of us has some regrets or fails to miss what once was. But what *is*…ah, it is so much better. And we no longer see one another with the eyes of deceit. Only the eyes of love.

We never met up with Timor again. In time, we stopped worrying about him. Constanze grows her flowers and keeps bees. She brews remedies to help our neighbors, who think of us only as a nice if fairly ordinary couple who live in the small cottage among the trees.

I gather firewood which I sell, and we make the best cheese in all the district.

We have our secrets, one of which I've seen fit to share with you. I used to be a Rat. Now I'm fortunate enough to be a Husband, and to live each day for the sake of love.

A word about the author…

A multi-award-winning author, Laura Strickland delights in time traveling to the past and searching out settings for her books, be they Historical Romance, Steampunk, or something in between.

Her first Scottish Historical hero, *Devil Black*, battled his way onto the publishing scene in 2013, and the author never looked back. Nor has she tapped the limits of her imagination. Venturing beyond Historical and Contemporary Romance, she created a new world with her ground-breaking Buffalo Steampunk Adventure series set in her native city, in Western New York.

Married and the parent of one grown daughter, Laura has also been privileged to mother a number of very special rescue dogs, and is intensely interested in animal welfare.

Her love of dogs, and her lifelong interest in Celtic history, magic and music, are all reflected in her writing. Laura's mantra is Lore, Legend, Love, and she wouldn't have it any other way.

Thank you for purchasing
this publication of The Wild Rose Press, Inc.

For questions or more information
contact us at
info@thewildrosepress.com.

The Wild Rose Press, Inc.